HIDE
and SEEK

Paul Brown

For mi Madre, for her unwavering love, faith and support

THE EXCELLENT EIGHT

Gavin Blair
Laura Cahill (nee O'Connor)
Colin Clark
Michelle Clark (nee Heron)
Steven Jenkins
Peter Perkins (Cas)
Peter Stevenson
Cheryl Stimson

CHAPTER 1

Gavin Blair sat on the armchair in his living room, hands gripped tightly on the armrests. Tears streamed down his cheeks. A flurry of images from the television played across his face and lit the room; the sound was muted. Beside him on the coffee table stood two tall glasses of cloudy water and a handwritten letter. His chest heaved as he fought back the tears. He felt the cold muzzle of a gun pressed against the back of his neck.

'It's time Gavin.'

'Please just let me go,' Gavin sobbed.

'I'm sorry. This is how it has to be done.'

'But why? I don't understand.'

'You're the starting point for the game.'

Gavin sniffed, choking back tears. He took a deep breath and summoned the last of his resolve.

'I won't do it. You'll just have to shoot me.'

He heard the gun being cocked ready to fire.

'This is your choice Gavin. But you're not saving anyone by doing it this way. The game will start regardless. You, Emma, Ben and Amy will have died for nothing.'

Gavin's lungs emptied of air in a huge rush as the tears came again.

'Please don't hurt them,' he said pitifully.

'This is your chance to save them Gavin. If you do what I ask I promise they will not be harmed in any way.'

'How can I trust you?'

'I don't need them to die Gavin, just you. You're the first domino that has to fall.'

'But why me first? Why not one of the others?'

'Because I know the ones who left town will come back for your funeral.'

Gavin shook his head. 'But why are you doing this now? After all these years?'

'Because something bad has happened again, and I never did get any justice for what the Excellent Eight did to start all of this.'

'I don't understand. You're one of the Excellent Eight.'

'But am I really?'

Gavin looked puzzled. He started to turn his head around but felt the muzzle of the gun push harder into the back of his neck. He tensed, expecting the worst.

'No more questions. You have ten seconds to drink up or I will shoot you right here. And then I'll wait until your wife and children come home and kill them too. 10......9......8.'

Gavin's hand shakily reached out and gripped the first glass. The countdown continued.

'7......6.......5.......'

Panic flowed throughout his body. He let out a final plea for mercy.

'*Please*, don't do this.'

The gun pressed even harder into the back of his neck, giving Gavin his answer as the countdown continued.

'4........3........'

Gavin knew it was futile. Images of his beautiful wife Emma and their two children flashed through his head. He held the glass to his lips. A few drops splashed into his mouth and left a bitter taste on his tongue.

'2.........1........'

Gavin tipped up the glass and the cloudy liquid flowed into his mouth. The taste was horrible and lingered in his mouth. He dry retched, his body shuddering uncontrollably. He placed the glass down on the table.

'Just one more and then you can go to sleep with the knowledge that you've saved your wife and children.'

Gavin picked up the second glass and held it in front of him. His panicked mind was jumbled with images and ideas, inhibiting him from forming a cohesive escape plan. For a second he thought he'd throw the glass at the far wall. He looked over to the mantelpiece which was adorned with family pictures. Tears continued to roll down his face. If he got rid of the glass what would that achieve? He'd already drunk one. Would one glass of crushed sleeping tablets kill him? Hell, he didn't even know if they *were* sleeping tablets. Still, he had heard all sorts of stories about people being found in time and having their stomachs pumped. But that wasn't going to happen here. He was going to die, if it wasn't the tablets it'd be a bullet to the head. The only difference was that if he didn't drink the second glass then his wife and children would be killed as well.

'Come on Gavin. You're half way there. No point in stopping now. '

His head hung resignedly. He looked down into the glass and noticed for the first time that the water was still fizzing slightly. It looked like a tiny geyser rising up from the middle of the glass, hitting the surface and causing ripples outwards to the edge where tiny lumps of the pills gathered together to form a ring.

'Gavin, do you really need another theatrical countdown?'

He took a deep breath, held the glass to his lips and started to glug the contents down. He dry retched again.

'Well done Gavin.'

He placed the glass back onto the coffee table.

'What happens now?'

'Move over to the couch and lie down. I'll stay with you until you fall asleep.'

Gavin rose heavily from the chair and immediately felt woozy, swaying a little on the spot. He couldn't tell whether it was the result of the emotional outpourings he had gone through or the pills starting to take effect. He stumbled forward and collapsed face first into the couch, turning over onto his side with difficulty. His eyes began watering and he blinked constantly. Through the blur he could see a pair of leather gloves picking up the letter from the coffee table.

'It might be my handwriting, but no one is going to believe I'd actually kill myself,' Gavin said.

'You'd be amazed what people will believe.'

'What are you going to do to the others? Are you going to kill them too?'

'We're all going to play a nice game of Hide and Seek, just like we did when we were kids.'

The words seemed slurred by the time they reached Gavin's brain, but he felt strangely comfortable lying on the couch. The nauseating panic he had felt earlier was ebbing away and he felt a little drunk. He didn't believe he was going to die. He was going to sleep and this was nothing but a bad dream. He tucked his hands under his armpits, nestled his head into the cushion and closed his eyes. He tried to speak but found that he was muttering incoherently.

'Sshhhh, go to sleep Gavin.'
They were the last words Gavin Blair ever heard.

CHAPTER 2
Sunday 25th November
11:58am

Peter Stevenson stood with his head bowed, arms clasped together in front of him as he watched the coffin being lowered into the ground.

His eyes roamed around the grounds of the cemetery, across the sea of tombstones and overgrown grass. He was surprised to see a gobstopper nestled on the dry mud of another recent grave. Peter looked up and away from the cemetery to a block of flats looming in the grey skies. He couldn't suppress a small smile. When he was a boy he, and the other members of the Excellent Eight, used to play a game where they would take it in turns to fire a gobstopper from the top floor of the flats to see who could get it the furthest. They would each cock the catapult to fire it up into the air and follow the downward trajectory as it fell into the grounds of the cemetery. Due to the appearance of this gobstopper, more than twenty years later, he wondered if a new generation of children were playing the same game.

Peter became conscious that he was smiling and guiltily looked around him at the crowd gathered around the grave but no one was looking at him. Each person stood the same way; hands clasped in front, heads bowed. Everything was quiet. He could only just make out the gentle hum of traffic. It was a stark reminder that people were getting on with their lives.

The priest stood at the top of the grave, like a father at the head of a table. He began his sermon, breaking the silence. Peter looked over at Gavin Blair's widow. Emma stood with her head bowed, her shoulders shuddering as she wept silently, her hands gripped tightly onto the shoulders of her two children. Ben and Amy stood solemnly by their mother. He was surprised that they were so well behaved, they were only six and four respectively but they seemed to know what was going on.

Peter continued to look around the crowd and his eyes met with Laura who was looking directly at him. She smiled shyly in acknowledgement and he returned the compassionate smile. He had spoken to his childhood sweetheart briefly before the funeral but it had only been small talk. If he was honest, it had been slightly awkward given the years that had passed without contact. In his communications with Gavin over the years, Peter hadn't asked much about Laura. Mainly because, like him, Laura had also moved away from the town, albeit a number of years after he did. Plus, he hadn't wanted to enquire about the first woman he had gone out with because it seemed a little obvious. However, she had stayed in touch with Michelle, and so Gavin had heard she got married six years ago, roughly around the same time Peter had married his wife Janine. Earlier today during their small talk he'd established that she had two children, six and four, the same age as Gavin's children. Peter remembered working out that she got married the same year as her first child was born and wondered if she only got married because she became pregnant. He felt annoyed at himself for creating his own gossip. They'd have more time to get reacquainted after the funeral. Perhaps he'd get the real story then.

Interrupting his train of thought, Peter heard a noise like someone knocking on a door. It seemed to be coming from inside the grave. Peter stared into the yawning gap in the grass. He could barely see the shape of the coffin in the low light of the overcast day. The priest continued to speak but his words became muffled like he was submerged in water. Peter focused on the knocking sound as it became louder and louder. He felt unable to breathe as he realised the sound was coming from inside the coffin.

Peter looked around the crowd for some acknowledgement that someone else could hear what he was hearing ... but nobody stirred. The knocking became more frantic and the muffled screams of his wife and son instantly made his heart jump. Peter instinctively ran forward and jumped into the grave landing on the coffin lid. He started trying to claw at the hinges but his fingers fumbled and slipped across the polished surface.

'Somebody help me!'

He stared up at the crowd gathered by the edge of the grave.

'Help me!' he shouted again but nobody moved.

His wife let out another terrified, muffled scream, 'Peter, help us.'

He continued to claw at the lid, aware that his fingers were scratched and dripping with blood. The bells of the church started to ring.

'Why won't anybody help me?' He screamed as the bells chimed louder.

6

The coffin lurched, moving away from him, disappearing further into the ground, yet he stayed in the same place. He strained with outstretched fingers as the coffin was swallowed into the darkness, out of his reach, beyond his grasp. He had lost them.

The sound of the bells was nearer now but they were no longer church bells.

Peter jolted awake and breathed a sigh of relief. He was hugging a pillow and lying sideways on a mattress, his legs spread like scissor blades. The sound of the alarm clock made him wince as he turned onto his back.

'Janine, turn off the alarm.'

His throat was dry and the words rasped out. He coughed to clear his throat, trying to find some saliva to wet his mouth. He heard no groaning response from his wife and the alarm continued to whine. He swung his left hand down to shake her shoulder but his hand clattered against a wooden panel instead. He groaned and rolled onto his side, searching for the soft warm body of his wife, but she was not there.

Peter lifted himself up in bed in a cumbersome manner. He massaged his forehead and rubbed his eyes with the palms of his hands. He surveyed the room as his eyes adjusted to the sparse light. He knew where he was supposed to be now, at Colin's house, sleeping in his spare room, but this wasn't Colin's house. He instantly felt anxious.

The annoying echo of the alarm clock reverberated in his brain intensifying his headache. He realised he was very low down and his right hand scrambled away from the mattress and touched the cold wooden floor. The walls around him were made of wood. He was in some kind of log cabin. He threw back the thin duvet cover and found that he was still wearing his suit from the funeral, including his shoes which were caked in mud. He stumbled onto his feet too quickly and felt dizzy. Groggily he fell forward managing to catch and steady himself on a bedside cabinet. His hands brushed along the surface eventually coming across the source of the incessant ringing. He fumbled with the small square travel clock in his hands like it was a Rubik's cube until he finally found and pushed the off switch and the beeping stopped.

Peter exhaled in relief as he was greeted with the wonderful sound of silence. Next to the cabinet was a window with the curtains closed. He grabbed them and threw them open. He squinted as the bright afternoon light streamed into his eyes. The sun was shining through rows of trees that stretched back as far as he could see.

'Where the hell am I?'

CHAPTER 3

12:01pm

Peter turned around and could see a door on the other side of the small room. He stumbled towards it and after rattling and wrestling with the old plastic handle it finally clicked into place and the door opened. The bedroom led out into the living room of the small cabin. Taking up the far corner at the back to his right was a sparse kitchen. To his right was another door. He peeked around and found a small bathroom with nothing more than a toilet, a sink with a dripping tap and a grimy bath. To his left he could see the doorway leading out into the woods. He tentatively crept out and peered around the corner beside the bedroom. There was a small space filled with a plastic covered couch overlooking another window. There was no television and no pictures on any of the walls.

'Hello?' He croaked.

There was no response. He walked over to the sink, turned on the tap, checked it with his fingers and cupped the water with both hands to drink greedily and wash his face. The water was cold on his face and woke him up. He massaged his forehead again; the headache continued to throb and it wasn't subsiding quickly enough for his liking. Something felt wrong. He'd obviously been hung-over before but this niggling headache and the dizziness he was experiencing didn't feel alcohol induced. Nor had he ever blacked out entire portions of a night before.

The last thing he could remember was that the remaining members of the Excellent Eight had left the post funeral gathering at the Oaktree pub and all gone back to Colin and Michelle's house. The mood had been surprisingly upbeat considering the sombre occasion, probably because the group of former childhood friends hadn't all been together in one place for over twenty years. They had dubbed themselves the 'Excellent Eight' when they were younger, mimicking the Enid Blyton series of books for The Famous Five and The Secret Seven.

Peter estimated that he could remember up until about 9pm but then the rest of the night was completely gone. A fleeting thought passed through his head. Had he tried any drugs? That was not like him. He'd tried a bit of weed during his university days, but nothing more than that. He did discover last night that Steve smoked a lot of weed and occasionally dabbled in ecstasy for nights out. He wondered if he had been drugged. He wouldn't put it past Steve to do something stupid like that.

Steven 'Joker' Jenkins loved to play pranks. He had always been a rascal in his youth and apparently this only got worse as he got older; and even more so after the breakup of his marriage. Peter had been told that his wife Lindsay was an extremely beautiful woman and Steve knew he was batting above his average with a girl like her. Hence when the whirlwind romance led to marriage, the birth of a child and divorce within the space of sixteen months Steve was diagnosed with clinical depression shortly after. The resulting counselling led to a rather flippant 'devil may care' attitude which meant that his pranks became more vicious, with less consideration for who he was hurting.

Peter had kept up with all the news on most of the Excellent Eight through Gavin Blair. They had stayed in touch over the years, sending the occasional letter, then email, and more recently through Facebook. They only messaged one another every couple of months; usually when either party was drunk and reminiscing about old days.

Peter had been as shocked as everyone when he found out that Gavin had committed suicide. Yesterday morning, whilst travelling on the train to Bilton for his funeral, Peter had spent the time looking back over old Facebook messages and emails on his mobile. He'd analysed them to see whether there was a cry for help which he'd missed, but he didn't find even the remotest forewarning that Gavin was suicidal.

Michelle had somehow managed to get Peter's phone number and rang to inform him of Gavin's death. She had also spoken with the other two who had left the town, Laura and Cas. Although it was obviously a melancholy occasion Michelle was insistent that this opportunity should be used to regroup the remaining seven members of the Excellent Eight in Gavin's honour. She and Colin volunteered to put up the three returning members. They had only recently moved into a new house in preparation for the arrival of their first baby, due in ten weeks time.

From what he could remember of last night, it had been going very well. Peter had been relieved that they had all instantly clicked, even after twenty years apart. They had spent the evening regaling each other with memories of their childhood days, and filling in the gaps with stories of what they'd been up to in the intervening years.

What happened after that? Why had he woken up in a cabin in the woods? Who did it belong to? If it was some kind of prank, why did they play it on him? He felt slightly annoyed that he might be the butt of their jokes and thought it was in bad taste. Anyway, it didn't look like there was anyone here who could give him answers. He'd have to make his way back to Colin and Michelle's house.

Peter jumped as the loud bleeping sound of an alarm rang out again from the bedroom and broke his train of thought.

'Damn it, I thought I turned that thing off.'

He went back into the bedroom, but the alarm wasn't coming from the travel clock that he'd turned off earlier. He followed the source of the noise and found a second clock tucked into the corner of the room. He picked it up and turned it off. It had been set for 12:05pm, five minutes after the first one. As he turned he noticed a third clock on a small shelf above the bedside cabinet. He walked over and pulled it down. The alarm was set for 12:10pm, he turned it off prematurely.

'Someone wanted to make sure I got up.'

He inspected his jacket pockets and then patted his trouser pockets. They were all empty. Where was his wallet, his mobile phone and keys?

'Shit.'

He searched diligently around the sparse bedroom and threw the duvet off the bed to check the mattress but couldn't find anything. He wondered if all his items might be back at Colin and Michelle's house. He stood there for a moment, wondering what to do. Peter felt uneasy, he had been trying to convince himself that this was a prank but it didn't make sense. He felt the overwhelming urge to get out of the cabin.

He came back out into the living room and was heading towards the front door when he saw a black metal ring handle laid flat across a door in the floor. The cabin must have a basement, he thought. He crouched down and pulled the ring to open the door half way. He stared down into the gaping black hole and shuddered. It reminded him of the grave from the nightmare he had just had.

He couldn't see anything, but a strong smell emanated from the basement. He scrunched up his face in disgust. It smelt like a cat litter tray which hadn't been emptied for a long time.

'Hello? Is anyone there?' He whispered down into the open mouth of the basement but nothing stirred and there was no reply.

He wondered if he should go down into the basement, if only to see what was causing the smell. He reasoned with himself that he had seen enough movies to know that when someone decided to investigate a creepy basement on their own, it usually didn't end well.

The door clattered as he closed it. He stood up and walked to the front door. With one hand on the handle he looked back one last time, panning the cabin with his eyes, and shook his head.

'What the hell is going on?'

CHAPTER 4

12:09pm

Peter opened the cabin door and walked outside. The early afternoon was cold and stark white, and a light frost twinkled on the grass. He walked away from the cabin onto the rough uneven ground and tried to get a bearing on his surroundings. He squinted and moved his head around trying to avoid the harsh light of the sun, which kept darting out from behind the cover of the trees. He looked for a landmark - anything recognisable - but all he could see were rows upon rows of trees, shed of their leaves from the autumn season that had just passed. He presumed that as long as he was still in Bilton that he must be in Durden Woods, which lay on the outskirts of the town. The Excellent Eight used to play games such as Hide and Seek in these woods when they were children, as well as build numerous elaborate dens. If this was some kind of prank how on earth had they got him way out here in the woods? He realised he had to find the walking trail which snaked through the middle of the woods and follow it to the exit. It was a guess, but he reckoned he was currently out on the east side of the woods and that he would have to head down into the middle to find the path. Without over thinking it too much he set off.

As he made his way through the woods he reflected on the nightmare he'd had earlier in the cabin. It was obviously based on the funeral he attended yesterday but the part with his wife and son trapped in the coffin disturbed him. He regretted not having his mobile phone because he hadn't spoken to Janine since early last night. Even though he had just been to a funeral she had still taken the time to playfully scold him for not replacing the tyres on their car. It had been taken in for a service a few weeks ago and the garage recommended new tyres because the tread was very low. He'd been so busy at work recently he kept putting it off, which had increasingly annoyed Janine but amused him simply because it wound her up so much.

He longed to talk to her now, to make sure she was alright. He wanted to hear his son, who would probably talk about the movie he was watching, completely unaware that his father was traipsing through some woods trying to work out how the hell he got there.

He felt a twinge of annoyance. If this was some kind of prank, probably headed up by Steve, it was irresponsible and dangerous to leave him in the middle of nowhere with no money and no way to contact anyone.

He thought about what he would do when he got back to Colin and Michelle's. Would he just smile and laugh along and congratulate them on the trick? Or would he find them at the house laughing at him as he arrived and get angry and shout at them? He wondered to himself if he might actually hit Steve and imagined the shock on the others' faces as he smashed his fist into Steve's jaw. As he thought about it he became more and more wound up. He tried to calm himself down and reasoned with himself that, in truth, he would probably be mainly relieved to find it was just a prank. He wondered if he was the only victim or whether any of the others had similarly woken up in some strange place.

Peter passed by a clump of trees and could see the walking trail in front of him. He smiled and congratulated himself. He'd always had a good sense of direction and of his surroundings which had helped him out on numerous occasions. He passed a large dead tree and joined the walking trail. The tree looked like a headless body sitting by the side of the trail. Two bulky roots spilled out onto the path resembling a pair of legs, with two brittle branches sprung from the side of the torso like arms reaching out.

'Creepy tree,' he said to himself.

Peter walked down the dusty trail of dried mud. His feet crunched on small pockets of frost. He put his hands in his pockets to keep them warm as he continued down the path.

Eventually Peter reached the end of the trail and jumped over the rickety wooden stile at the edge of the woods and came out onto the hills. From this vantage point he could see the entire layout of the town.

Bilton was a post-industrial town with a population of around 20,000. To his right he could see the desolated industrial estate, which used to teem with various businesses, and the mill factory that stood behind it. The tall thin chimneys of the factory used to pour out smoke continuously like lit cigarettes but now just stood there looking lonely. The town had been built in the '70s and expanded in the '80s to accommodate the rising workforce. It was a self-sufficient town then but after the factory closed it had withered away to nothing. Peter thought that if the town of Bilton was being advertised for sale like a house, the description would read something like:

'Starter home, needs modernising, a good investment opportunity.'

The entire town lay in a valley, nestled in the bosom of hills which swept around the entire north, east and west side of the town in the shape of a horse shoe. From his position at the top of the hill Peter felt like he was looking into a goldfish bowl. He knew from his childhood that the overbearing hills surrounding the town gave it a claustrophobic feel. The town felt closed in and small and yet it was a maze of estates and shops riddled with little nooks and crannies hiding all sorts of things for people to find.

At the bottom of the hill ran Wolviston Road, which began at the industrial estate to his right. It followed the line of the hills and then curled into town towards Colin and Michelle's house.

Peter made his way down the hill, crossed the small field at the bottom and started making his way to the house.

Peter walked along Wolviston Road, past Bilton Beck and entered the housing estate. The houses had passed him by in a blur as he trudged along with his head down. He was feeling especially grumpy from all the walking and the gnawing headache, which still persisted. His forehead was clammy and lined with perspiration.

It was still concerning him that he couldn't remember anything from about 9pm the previous night. He had been hoping that by now he would have been able to recount something, anything to jog his memory, but it was completely gone, like a wiped hard drive. He was looking forward to reaching Colin and Michelle's house and getting some answers.

CHAPTER 5

12:48pm

Peter arrived at 69 South Road. It was a detached building on a decent stretch of land. Three cars were parked on the driveway leading up to a double garage. He knew that two of them belonged to Colin and Michelle and the other was a black and silver Vauxhall Tigra with the personalised number plate of L4 URA. Peter had mentioned this to Laura last night and she had smiled coyly saying she didn't like it because she thought it was pretentious but it had been a birthday gift from her husband. He remembered thinking that it revealed a lot about her husband if he would buy something like that for her which she obviously hadn't asked for.

He wondered why Laura was still here. Last night she'd said she was leaving early as she had to be home by noon. A part of him hoped it was to see him before she left. Then again, he couldn't remember anything of last night so had no idea what plans might have been changed. Maybe she'd found out about the prank and was waiting to make sure he got back safely from the woods. He hoped she'd had no involvement in this prank. Even if she did, he was glad she was still here. He wanted to see her just once more before they parted company for what could be another twenty years.

He suddenly felt conscious of his appearance. He knew he looked like shit but he couldn't really do anything about it until he got in the house and cleaned himself up.

Peter walked up the path and knocked on the door. He looked searchingly through the glass for signs of movement in the hallway or on the stairway straight ahead but there was nothing.

He tried the door handle and found the door was open. He slowly peered in, and shouted out 'Hello?' but there was no answer.

On a table next to the door he found a handwritten note which read 'Peter wait here.' The note was signed by Colin and had a mobile number underneath the signature.

A stale smell of smoke and alcohol filled the air. He crossed over the laminated hallway into the living room, which had a through lounge stretching all the way to the back of the house. This was the last place he remembered being last night. The room was littered with beer bottles, cans and half full glasses of wine. The living room led through into the kitchen out of his sight. A slight mist of smoke crept out of the kitchen, twisting and whirling, illuminated by the light streaming through the French patio doors.

Peter walked back across the hallway to the study and crossed the room to go through a door leading into the kitchen. Again, there were more signs of the party which had taken place last night. He felt concerned. He wasn't sure how house-proud Colin and Michelle were but he thought that some tidying up would have commenced this morning, even if it was just putting the cans in the bin and gathering the bottles so they could be put into the recycling bin later. The house looked like it had been abandoned.

He decided to venture up the stairs shouting out again, 'Hello?' with no answer.

The first floor landing had three bedrooms leading off it on one side and two bathrooms on the other side. Peter explored each of the rooms. The bed in the master bedroom was undisturbed and all the curtains were open. Either the bed had been made up this morning or no one had slept in it last night. He checked the second bedroom which he and Cas were supposed to share.

As there were two Peter's in the group, Peter Perkins was nicknamed Cas in reference to Casper the Friendly Ghost, because of his pale ghostly complexion.

It had been agreed last night that Cas would get the bed and Peter would take the sleeping bag on the floor. Cas was a big man with a rugby player's build so he got the bed by default with no argument from Peter. Again, the bed was undisturbed although he was relieved to see his travel bag in the corner of the room where he'd dumped it yesterday morning. Cas' bags were still there too. He checked the third bedroom which had been allocated to Laura. Again, the bed was undisturbed and her travel bags were sat on top of the bed. He quickly checked the bathrooms but they were empty too, as he'd suspected they might be.

Peter went downstairs into the living room. He stood still for a moment wondering what to do. He spotted a landline phone perched on the windowsill. He retrieved the note from the hallway and rang the hand-written number. A mobile phone started ringing in the kitchen. He left the phone off the hook and went into the kitchen, followed the noise and opened the drawer from which the noise was coming.

'That's just great. Well done Colin,' he said sarcastically.

He returned to the living room with the mobile and placed the landline phone back on its receiver to halt the annoying William Tell ringtone of Colin's mobile phone. How stupid did you have to be to put your mobile number on a note for someone and actually forget to take your phone with you? He put the mobile phone on the mantelpiece and picked up the landline phone again and rang his own mobile. As it dialled he hoped he would hear it ring somewhere in the house but he heard nothing and it went straight to voicemail. He hung up, frustrated.

'How very irksome.'

CHAPTER 6

13:03pm

Peter climbed the stairs and went into the second room and sat on the undisturbed bed, exhaling loudly in relief as he kicked off his muddied shoes. He stripped out of his clothes, retrieved a towel and his toiletry bag and crossed the landing to the bathroom. He looked at the dishevelled man staring back at him. His eyes were slightly bloodshot, his skin looked blotchy and his mousy brown hair was ruffled and was sticking up on the right side.

'Yep, you look like shit.'

He patted his stomach, pleased at how it was still well defined. He liked to keep fit and kept the flab at bay with a twice weekly routine of squash. However, unpredictable work patterns had wrecked his routine over the last year so he was surprised that it still looked like he was taking care of himself even though he knew he wasn't. He had a relief-filled piss and then brushed his teeth. He debated whether to have a shave but decided he couldn't be bothered. He stepped into the shower, the hot water was invigorating and for ten minutes he just stood there with his head bowed under the nozzle letting the water massage and revitalise his body.

He left the bathroom and stood in the hallway, listening in case anyone had come into the house whilst he was in the shower. The house was still deathly quiet. He returned to the second bedroom and dried off. The feeling of fresh clothes was, again, refreshing and he bagged up the dirty clothes and packed his travel bag up. He was starting to feel a little agitated. He was booked on the 3:12pm train and it was twenty minutes from here by taxi to the station. His plan was to wait for the others to come back, get a quick debrief on what the hell happened last night, then he'd get a taxi to the station and have a full English breakfast at the greasy spoon cafe he spotted on his way here, before boarding the train for home. His stomach gurgled as if agreeing with his plan.

Peter relaxed in the chair in the front room, thinking about last night's events, trying again to recap as much as he could for some clue as to what was going on. He rubbed his eyes and brow, still feeling hazy, the dull headache *still* there. Had he been drugged or taken drugs? He couldn't imagine any scenario, no matter how drunk he was, in which he would be convinced to take drugs. He was still feeling tired and his eyes stung a little at the stark white light of the early afternoon sun streaming in through the open blinds. He thought he'd rest his eyes for a while.

A knock at the door startled him awake. It had only felt like a few seconds but a quick check of the clock on the mantelpiece revealed he must have dozed off for at least ten minutes. He groggily rose from the chair and looked out of the window - a police car was parked on the driveway. An immediate feeling of panic swept over him and he rushed to answer the door.

Peter recognised the officer immediately. It was the town's Chief Superintendent, who also happened to be Michelle's father. He wasn't wearing his police uniform but he still had an authoritarian presence. He always reminded Peter of the actor Sam Elliot because of his flowing grey hair and the white moustache which sat permanently on his upper lip. It was the moustache, and his tendency to wear a cowboy hat when out of uniform, which had led to him being dubbed 'The Sheriff' - he seemed like a throwback from an old western. As children they joked that he would probably have put spurs on his boots and wore a holster if he had been allowed to.

'Hello Mr Heron,' Peter said timidly.

He felt himself returning to childhood and being shyly polite around his friends' parents. The Sheriff's face softened as he inspected him and a flash of recognition passed over his face.

'Peter Stevenson? Well well, how are you?'

Peter smiled and without checking himself replied, 'I'm okay Sheriff.'

Peter stopped himself, realising what he'd said. The Sheriff simply smiled. He was obviously aware of the nickname and Peter could tell that he wasn't displeased with the moniker.

Peter moved to one side and The Sheriff walked into the house and through to the living room as Peter followed. He surveyed the carnage of the party and turned back to Peter.

'Where is everyone?'

Peter responded, 'I'm not sure.'

The Sheriff looked at him quizzically, clearly not impressed with his answer.

The Sheriff probed further, 'Are you the only one here?'

It was clear that he was aware that Colin and Michelle were putting the three outsiders up and was confused as to why he was the only one in the house. Peter felt uncomfortable and a sense of guilt came over him; it always seemed to happen when he talked to police officers even though he'd done nothing wrong. Although a thought flashed through his mind - because he had no idea what he got up to last night - that might not necessarily be true on this occasion. Peter really felt like he didn't want to talk about waking up in a cabin in the middle of Durden Woods because even in his own head it sounded strange and was bound to lead The Sheriff to probe for more information. Information he didn't have.

'Yes. I didn't end up sleeping here last night and I just got back about half an hour ago.'

The Sheriff raised his eyebrows and Peter realised that his lack of description sounded even more suspicious, and perhaps suggested that he had slept at a woman's house. Peter ignored the obvious look from The Sheriff for more details.

'I lost my phone last night so I haven't been able to ring anyone. I think they all went for lunch or something. Colin left a note.'

He retrieved the note from the mantelpiece and handed it to The Sheriff. A perplexed look came over his face. The Sheriff took his mobile phone out of his pocket and his finger scrolled over the Smartphone, his eyes moved back and forth from the note to his phone.

'This isn't Colin's mobile number.'

CHAPTER 7

13:44pm

'What?' Peter replied as The Sheriff started to dial the number on the note.

The Sheriff continued, 'It doesn't even look like his handwriting,' he added.

Peter knew that the mobile phone on the mantelpiece would start ringing and he retrieved it and handed it to The Sheriff.

'No need to ring it, the phone is right here, I found it in the kitchen.'

'Is this your phone?'

Peter looked at The Sheriff as if he had just asked the stupidest question in the world.

'No, it's not mine. Maybe it belongs to one of the others. Maybe Colin lost his phone and borrowed one of the others.'

'There seems to be a lot of phones that got lost last night,' The Sheriff said in a matter-of-fact manner.

Peter could only nod and agree, offering up a vague, 'we all got pretty drunk last night.'

'And you don't know who could have written this?'

'No, I don't know what Colin's writing is like. Are you sure it isn't his?'

'I've signed off enough of his reports to recognise his writing.'

They both stood silent for a few moments each pondering on their own thoughts. Peter, now more than ever, was feverishly trying to recap last night's events. The Sheriff broke the silence with an obvious statement.

'This seems a little odd.'

Peter nodded.

The Sheriff continued. 'Colin didn't show up for work this morning. Not that I was surprised but I've been ringing him all morning and he hasn't replied. That's why I came over. I just assumed he'd be laid in bed nursing a hangover again.'

Colin worked on the police force under his father-in-law. When Peter had spoken to Colin about this last night it was apparent that the two of them didn't get along particularly well. Apparently, The Sheriff had told Colin on more than one occasion that he was a 'stupid lazy bastard'.

The Sheriff returned to the role of a concerned father for his next question.

'Michelle isn't answering her phone either. Was she drinking last night?'

Peter felt uneasy with the interrogative nature of the question, as if he was trying to catch him out.

'No, I think she might have had one glass of wine but that was it.'

'I take it from the mess that you all came back here. What time did you leave them last night?'

Peter avoided the question.

'We were all at the Oaktree straight after the funeral, and then we came back here.'

The Sheriff was distracted by the mention of the funeral. He nodded humbly.

'It was very tragic what happened to Gavin. Everyone was very shocked. It's a shame, he was a good man.'

The Sheriff didn't seem noticeably emotional when he spoke and Peter wondered if he even knew Gavin or whether he was merely being polite. He immediately changed the subject.

'Who came back here after the pub?'

'Everyone. Colin, Michelle, me, Cas,' he paused. 'I mean Peter Perkins.'

The Sheriff nodded in recognition of the name.

Peter continued, 'Laura O'Connor, Cheryl Stimson and Steve Jenkins.'

The Sheriff took a second to recall Laura from the past but then nodded again.

'Steven? Steven came back here?'

'Yes,' Peter responded slightly curious as to the reason why he would single Steve out, as if he was surprised that Steve came back to the house.

The Sheriff scrolled his finger over his phone again and started ringing someone. He held the phone to his ear, waited for a few seconds and then sighed and hung up.

'Voicemail as well.'

Peter assumed it was Steve he'd called. The Sheriff stood for a few seconds, obviously having an internal debate.

'Right,' he said determined, 'I'm going to try Steven's house first, the Oaktree pub is on the way so I'll pop in and see if they're there. Are you going to join me?'

Peter felt like it would probably be the best thing to do, as The Sheriff was more likely to find the others and he could then get his wallet, phone and keys and head to the train station. However, the uncomfortable feeling of being around someone who was both a police officer and a parent persisted within him. If he was honest he wanted to be away from The Sheriff's company as soon as possible, to avoid any further awkward questioning.

'No thanks. I need to catch a train in about an hour so I better wait here in case they turn up whilst you're out looking for them.'

'Alright then, well hopefully one of us can find them in time for you to get that train back home.'

'Hopefully.'

'If they do come back here tell my daughter to call me straight away.'

'Sure. I will do.'

The Sheriff walked out of the house and gave Peter some final words.

'You bloody kids, never grow up, always playing games.'

He continued muttering to himself as he strolled up the path towards his car. Peter stood alone in the living room for a few minutes going over the conversation he'd just had. Numerous questions flashed through his mind, coupled with a dark sense of foreboding as he recounted the day so far.

He had woken up in a strange cabin in the middle of Durden Woods. He had a gnawing headache and felt like he'd been drugged. He had returned to Colin and Michelle's house. Laura's car was still here so she hadn't left early like she had planned to. No one was in the house and it looked like it had been abandoned mid-party. No one seemed to be contactable by phone. The only clue that had been left was a note signed by Colin, but according to The Sheriff wasn't written by Colin. And the note had a mobile number for a phone that had been left in the house and apparently didn't belong to Colin either. Who did the phone belong to? It was a relatively old Nokia.

Peter jumped as the phone rumbled in his hand, the display lit up and the William Tell tone started playing. The caller ID flashed up with the message 'Peter Stevenson calling.'

CHAPTER 8

14:00pm

Peter stared in disbelief at the ringing phone for a few seconds and then answered it with an uncertain 'Hello?'

There was silence at the other end of the line for a further few seconds and then a metallic electronic voice rang out.

'Hello Peter. How's your head this morning?'

Peter felt a little perturbed by the distorted voice but immediately assumed that it was Steve playing another practical joke. He decided he would go along with it although he was really not in the mood for more games and the fact that he had to catch his train in an hour was playing heavily on his mind.

'My head's a little hazy. We must have drunk a lot Steve. I feel like I was drugged. I can hardly remember anything about last night. What...'

The disembodied voice interrupted him.

'You *were* drugged. The hazy head and eye stinging is an after effect.'

A creeping suspicion that the person on the phone was not Steve entered his mind.

'What do you mean I was drugged?'

'I had to get you out of the way for a few hours whilst I set up the game.'

Peter felt himself becoming angry, if this was another of Steve's jokes he was seriously not in the mood.

'What game? What are you on about? Who is this?'

'You can call me Celo.'

Peter searched his mind for some relevance to the name but drew a blank. As if reading his mind Celo elaborated.

'It's Latin, meaning to hide, conceal, keep secret.'

Peter responded half-heartedly and a little sarcastically, he was quickly boring of this game.

'Okay, that's nice.'

'I thought that seeing as though all seven surviving members of the Excellent Eight are in town, that we should all play a game just like we used to.'

Peter could feel his agitation levels creeping up again.

'I haven't got time for this shit. I have to catch a train in an hour. I'm not playing any games with you.'

The electronic voice snapped back furiously, 'You will play the game or all your friends will die.'

The sudden outburst stunned Peter into silence. Then Celo lowered his tone, regained composure and spoke again calmly.

'Listen carefully. We are going to play a game of Hide and Seek. Do you remember we all used to love playing that?'

Peter didn't respond.

'Well, the other six members of the Excellent Eight are hidden in separate places within the town and you, Peter Stevenson, are the seeker. They are hidden in places where we played as children and I'll give you a clue to find each one of them. But you only have a certain amount of time to find them. If you take too long to find any individual person then I'm afraid that member will die.'

Peter's head was awash with scrabbled thoughts, unable to fully comprehend what was being said to him. He was still half hoping that this was some form of elaborate hoax. Again, as if reading his mind, Celo went on.

'I realise that this is a lot to take in. And that you might be half hoping this is still just one of Steve's pranks. So I'd like you to check the oven in the kitchen. That should put to rest any doubts you have about the seriousness of the game. I'll call you back in a few minutes with further instructions.'

The phone went silent as Celo hung up, leaving Peter standing on the spot with the phone pressed against his ear, knuckles white. He turned and looked towards the kitchen with trepidation and slowly started to walk towards it. He placed the phone on the kitchen work surface and stared at the oven wondering what could be inside. Before he knew it he realised one of his own hands was clenching the cool handle of the oven door. He tensed and squinted as he started to pull the handle down, dropping down on one knee to look inside, not knowing what to expect, as if a bomb might go off in his face.

Inside the dark oven he could see a baking tray. Something sat in the middle of it. He pinched two fingers like tweezers and carefully gripped the edges of the baking tray. He was half expecting it to be hot but the oven was off, the tray cold. As his fingers investigated he felt the distinctive crumpled shiny surface of foil lining the tray. He started to edge it out onto the open oven door and could see a pool of thick black oil around the outskirts of the object. He realised that it was not oil, but congealed blood. He pulled the tray out fully. Sat in the middle was a dismembered arm, the skin discoloured with a slightly blue and purple tint. The arm had been cut off at the elbow joint, the knuckles white and blue on the clenched fist.

Peter stumbled back on himself in shock, knocking the tray. It flipped over and off the side of the oven door and the arm landed with a sickening wet thud as spatters of congealed blood splashed across the floor. The tray noisily clattered on the tiles. He shimmied backwards away from the mess, his back bumping heavily into the legs of the kitchen table, his eyes transfixed on the bloodied arm. His stomach shuddered and he retched as the smell filtered into his nostrils. He jumped to his feet and crouched over the sink, retching again. He fumbled with the tap and splashed water in his face and grabbed cupfuls of water to drink. He looked down at the bloodied arm and his heart dropped as he saw a tattoo inked into the underside of the arm which read 'The long arm of the law' in italic writing. It was the same tattoo that Colin had shown them last night.

Peter remembered that Colin had challenged Cas to an arm wrestle. Colin had always been a slim child with no muscles but through his time with the police force he'd bulked up considerably. Colin rolled back his shirt sleeve and propped his arm on the table goading Cas to prove he was still the arm wrestling champion of the group. Cas accepted the challenge and clasped hands with Colin. Michelle, Cheryl and Laura rolled their eyes at the stereotypical male bravado.

'Boys will always be boys,' Cheryl chided, but the men ignored her.

Peter could see that Colin already had doubts simply from the grip Cas had on him. Cas knew this too and as they waited for Steve to count them down he looked into Colin's eyes and smiled. The contest was over in a matter of seconds.

'Not bad Col, but not good enough.'

Colin's pride was obviously wounded but he accepted his defeat with good humour.

'I'll get you one of these days.'

Cas then spotted the ink on the underside of Colin's exposed arm. Colin explained that he and four of his colleagues had all got the same tattoo on the day they graduated.

Peter shakily pulled a chair out from the kitchen table and slumped into it, breathing out heavily to try and control his nausea. He looked down again at the arm laid in the pool of blood. The open wound at the elbow joint was facing towards him and he was surprised how neat the cut was. From years of watching gory horror movies he had expected veins to be hanging out like entrails but it looked like it had been sliced through cleanly. Questions were jumbling through his mind like a washing machine. He couldn't concentrate on answering one question before another tumbled along. Where was the rest of Colin? Was he still alive?

Peter jumped as the mobile phone emitted a hum and started to rattle on the work surface and a second later the William Tell ringtone began to echo out again.

CHAPTER 9

14:09pm

Peter lifted himself up from the chair, his hand stretched out on the table giving him extra support, his legs weak. He felt like he was learning to walk again. He stumbled around the dismembered arm cautiously, as if it might suddenly come to life and lunge at him. He scrambled for the phone, never taking his eyes off the arm.

The metallic electronic voice spoke.

'Now you know why Colin's handwriting looked a little different on the note left for you.'

'Why are you doing this?'

'I told you, we're playing a game. Don't worry; the rest of Colin is alive and well. For now at least. But as you've probably guessed that all depends on you Peter. There's something in Colin's clenched hand which will help you with the game.'

Peter stared down at the white knuckles of the clenched fist.

'Now we should go over the rules of the game. Are you listening Peter? Are you focussed?'

'Yes,' Peter muttered.

'Good. The rules are quite simple. You must keep this phone with you at all times. It is the only way I will contact you and the only way you can receive the clues that will help you find each member of the Excellent Eight. Do you understand?'

'Yes,' Peter said quietly, he felt like a child being told off by a teacher. Celo continued.

'I notice that you've already reacquainted yourself with The Sheriff but be warned that this game is for members of the Excellent Eight only. No grown-ups allowed. You will not involve anyone else in the game or tell them anything about me. If you do it will be considered an immediate forfeit and the game will be null and void. For the purposes of clarification, if you involve anyone else in this game *all* the players *will* die. If you involve the police or are questioned by the police *all* the players *will* die. Do you understand Peter?'

'Why are you doing this?'

Celo ignored the question and persisted.

'Do you understand the rules of the game Peter?'

Peter responded resignedly.

'Yes, I understand.'

'Good, then here is your first clue. It's a place where you used to go with the boys and the girls. Stacked houses so high they touch the sky. Don't play on the stairs or you will cry. Colin Clark has bad memories of this place.'

Peter looked blankly at the window as he gripped the phone tightly.

'What? I don't understand.'

Celo responded, 'Think about it Peter, I'm sure you'll remember. You have until three o'clock to find and save him, the game starts … *now*.'

Celo paused for a second and then added 'Ready or not.'

The phone call ended and Peter was left staring blankly at the window, the phone gripped tightly in one hand. His arm dropped to his side as he swung giddily on the spot. He felt sick. What was he going to do?

He thought first of Colin, and then about the other members of the Excellent Eight. He was the seeker, Gavin was dead, and then there was Cas, Laura, Colin, Michelle, Cheryl and Steve. This maniac had six of his friends. He ran through to the living room and to the front bay window, as if for some reason The Sheriff would still be there but of course he wasn't. He looked down at the phone in his hand. A voice was shouting in his head for him to call the police but Celo's words were louder. 'If you involve the police or are questioned by the police all the players will die,' he had said. Who could he ring? Who could he trust? Would Celo find out? Was he watching him right now? All of a sudden it felt like the room had gone icy cold as he looked around the foreign surroundings. He looked towards the kitchen, and thought of the severed arm lying on the floor, Colin's arm.

Peter tried to rationalise the thoughts flying through his mind. Celo knew that Peter had met The Sheriff, which had to mean he must be watching the house. He looked through the front bay window again and stared out onto the street. Opposite Colin and Michelle's house were a couple of shops with flats above them. Was he hiding in one of them, watching him right now? But Celo had mentioned the handwriting on the note exactly as if he had heard what The Sheriff and him had discussed. Perhaps the house was bugged?

Peter started to frantically search for something that would confirm this, lifting magazines, looking inside lightshades, checking under the sofa and the armchairs. He found nothing.

'This is useless.'

He didn't really know what he was looking for. What did a bug look like? And even if he did find a bug, what would that tell him? Nothing he didn't already know. He sat down on the floor, rubbing his fingers through his scalp, exhaling loudly to try and calm the feeling of nausea in his stomach. Who would have access to bugging equipment? The first answer to his own question was the very people he wanted to call right now.

'The police.'

Then he closed his mouth suddenly in realisation that if the house was bugged Celo could hear him right now. Peter stood up. He started shuffling on the spot with nervous energy, as if this would make him think more clearly. The police have bugging equipment, he thought. Colin might have access to bugging equipment from the station. And then he stopped suddenly on the spot. What if it was The Sheriff? Would he really come round to check on two grown-ups? Even if they were family? But then, why would he be doing this? What would he have against his own son-in-law? Except for thinking he was a 'stupid lazy bastard' not good enough for his daughter. And why would he involve his daughter in this? What could he have against the members of the Excellent Eight? His mind flicked back to The Sheriff's reaction when he had mentioned Steve coming back to the house. He had seemed surprised by that. He'd then phoned Steve. Why would The Sheriff have Steve's mobile number? His finger hovered over the 9 button to dial 999. He hesitated. Something was bugging him about The Sheriff's reaction to Steve coming back to the house.

He remembered a conversation last night when Cas had asked him whether he'd noticed anything strange going on between Steve and Michelle. Peter hadn't noticed anything untoward and hadn't realised what Cas was suggesting at the time but the question had led him to watch the pair more closely. He'd then noticed that they didn't speak to each other directly all night; as if they were avoiding each other. But he had also caught them looking at each other when they thought other people's attention was elsewhere. Something must have happened between Steve and Michelle. He had no idea when they had slept together, or whether they were still sleeping together or whether Colin knew about it. Whenever Peter caught Steve and Michelle looking at each other, he would look straight away to Colin but he didn't seem aware of anything and kept himself engrossed in conversation with the others. A sickening thought entered his mind. He recalled a conversation between the group when they had all returned to Colin and Michelle's house. The conversation had turned onto the topic of babies. He and Laura had dispensed their wisdom and advice based on their own parenting experiences. They had also simultaneously confirmed the common mantra, as a light-hearted warning, that Colin and Michelle's life would never be the same once the baby was born. Peter recalled that Colin had proudly patted his wife's stomach with a wide smile.

'I don't care, I'll just be glad when she's here. We've wanted a baby so long. We'd almost given up and then boom, it just happened.'

Peter recalled the smile on Michelle's face. It had not been a beaming grin of pride. He'd initially thought it was a shy smile at the fact that Colin had been rather upfront and given slightly too much detail about their obvious struggles to have a child. Now he realised he might have misinterpreted it; that it was, in fact, a nervous smile of guilt. He now wished he'd looked at Steve to gauge his reaction to the comments.

'Jesus Christ.'

He wondered if Michelle had confessed her sins to her father, The Sheriff. His finger moved away from the 9 button and he put the phone on the mantelpiece. He slumped down into the armchair. He put his head in his hands as conspiracy theories emerged from hidden corners of his mind, like people whispering in the shadows of a dark alleyway.

His mind flashed back to reality as if he had slammed the door shut to escape the whispering conspiracies. He had almost forgotten about the immediate threat to Colin. He picked up the phone to look at the time, the display read 14.18pm. He only had 42 minutes to find Colin. He wondered what would happen if he didn't get there on time. Would Colin really be killed? He wasn't certain, but thinking about the severed arm, it was a possibility.

He tried to recall the clue from Celo.

'A place where you used to go with the boys and the girls. Okay, that means it must be somewhere where we used to play as kids. Stacked houses so high they touch the sky?'

There was only one place that could be.

CHAPTER 10

14:19pm

The Excellent Eight used to play games at Bilton flats, which lay on the outskirts of the town near the primary school he'd gone to. The flats had been built in the late '70s and even when he was a kid they already looked old. There were ten floors to the flats and twelve apartments on each floor. The top two floors were no longer occupied; back in '88 a storm damaged the roof and the rain had got in and completely ruined the top floor flats and sufficiently dampened the floors to affect the ceilings of the 9th floor as well. The roof had been repaired but the rooms had never been renovated because there wasn't enough demand for the eight remaining floors anyway. Therefore, this is where the kids usually played.

The rest of the clue then made perfect sense to him.

Don't play on the stairs or you will cry. Colin Clark has bad memories of this place.

The Excellent Eight had been playing on the 10th floor. They'd been catapulting gobstoppers from an empty apartment window to see who could get it the furthest. The lifts weren't working and so they were coming down one of the stairways. They took it in turn to run and jump down entire flights. Sometimes over-jumping and smashing into the walls. By the time they reached the last three flights of stairs they were tired. Steve decided to start sliding down the banister railings and went flying down fast but perfectly dismounted at the end like a gymnast coming off a pommel horse. Colin decided to copy Steve and slid down on his front, balls first. He caught his leg on the corner of the railings, span off the banister and threw his hands out to protect himself. He fell onto the next flight of stairs and bounced down them to the floor below. It all happened so fast, everybody was stunned into silence.

Steve eventually shouted out 'Colin!'

Then they heard the shocked sobbing begin.

The group ran down the stairs. They found Colin sat upright against the wall holding his right hand with his left. He looked up as they came down the stairs, his eyes red and wet, tears streaming down his face. His cheeks were covered in little cuts but those were minor, the major concern was the angle at which his hand was pointing. It was obvious straight away that he had broken it and the group quickly helped him home. Colin's mother was ironing clothes when they arrived and as soon as she reacted he started to cry again. The group had to endure both interrogation and scolding from Colin's mother but it was mercifully brief as she realised that she needed to get him to the hospital. The group stood and watched as Colin, feeling very sorry for himself, was driven away.

Peter considered his options for getting to the flats. He had no car and no money for a taxi. Celo presumably had his wallet, which removed a lot of his options. It was all part of his sick game not to make it too easy for him to get around. He reckoned it was at least a twenty-five minute walk. He could probably make it in fifteen minutes if he ran, although he knew that he wasn't in the best of shape and even though Colin's life depended on him, he knew he probably couldn't run for fifteen minutes flat. Peter remembered that Colin and Michelle's cars were parked on the driveway. There had to be spare keys somewhere, perhaps even some money.

His eyes darted around the living room and spotted a chest of drawers. He rifled through each drawer looking for anything that could be useful but they were full of letters, bills, pictures and old telephone directories. He ran upstairs and began a frenzied search through the wardrobes and cupboards in each of the bedrooms. He could find nothing of use and so he made his way back downstairs and went into the study. Peter continued his search through the drawers of the computer table but was already beginning to feel panicked; worried that this was a futile exercise that was wasting precious time. His last attempt was the kitchen. He ran in, completely forgetting about the severed arm in the middle of the floor, and stopped dead in his tracks. He decided to abandon searching the kitchen and walked back into the living room. He had just wasted at least ten minutes searching through the house and he was no further forward. He had to leave now and get to the flats - time was running out.

He made his way towards the door and then suddenly recalled what Celo had said on the phone. There was something in Colin's clenched hand, something which would help him with the game. He crossed back into the kitchen and knelt down by the arm. The stench of the already decomposing flesh stung his nostrils. He held his nose with one hand as he prodded the clenched fist with a finger cautiously, as if it might scurry away like Thing from The Addams Family. But the hand was cold to the touch and stiff. What was it concealing? As he moved his head closer to inspect, he saw a glint of metal through a small gap between the fingers. He decided to approach the task like the principle behind taking off a plaster. He would do it as quickly as possible. He took a deep breath and held it. He gripped the upper wrist steady with one hand and used his other to prise the stiff fingers away from the palm. The fingers came away one by one. He baulked every time he heard the sickening snap of bone at the knuckle and finger joints. After he had prised the third finger away he could see a key ring holding three keys nestled in the palm of Colin's hand. He grabbed at them and pulled them briskly away, then ran back into the living room. He emptied his lungs of the air he had been holding and took in a deep breath now that he was away from the stench of the dismembered arm.

He looked down at the keys wondering what they could be used for. For one of the cars on the driveway he hoped, but he could see now that they were all Yale lock keys. He rattled them in the palm of his hand and noticed that one key had the number nine engraved on it. He thought for a second, was there anything in the house that could be unlocked with one of these? He couldn't think of anything.

Peter picked up the mobile phone from the mantelpiece. He read the time on the display. He had to go *now*; too much time had been wasted here already. He grabbed his jacket, shoved the phone and the keys in a pocket - took a final brief pause by the front door - then took a deep breath and set off.

CHAPTER 11

14:36pm

Peter walked out onto the main road. He felt jittery and jumpy; the sounds of the outside world all seemed jumbled together chaotically. It had been quiet inside Colin and Michelle's house but now the sounds of cars, the gusting wind, the beeping of a pedestrian crossing, all ordinary sounds which now seemed suddenly noticeable and extremely loud. He took a look up at the buildings opposite the house, his mind playing with the thought that Celo could be behind one of those windows right now watching him. He shuddered as he turned and walked up to the junction. He stood at the corner watching the traffic go by, waiting for a break to cross the road. He felt like he was in the middle of a time lapse movie and everything was speeded up and rushing past him.

The air was cold, sudden erratic bursts of the whistling wind ruffled his clothes and bit at his exposed skin. The stark white light of the afternoon was fading and quickly being replaced by grey skies dotted with dark clouds. He didn't know if it had actually got colder or whether he was trembling through fear. He zipped up his jacket as he felt a light spray of rain brush across his face. He crossed the junction and started walking briskly up the street, almost jogging. The path ahead was a long road on a steep incline that cut straight up through the west side of the town. At the top of the road he knew there was a busy three way junction. If he turned right he'd be at the entrance to the high street which snaked diagonally down through the centre of town. He had to continue straight on at the junction towards the northwest of the town, which lay at the foot of the hills. He would head towards the primary school and continue past it to the flats at the end of a cul-de-sac.

As he passed people on the street, they seemed to stare at him. And the further he walked, the more his paranoia grew. He felt as if everyone was watching him. A thought crossed his mind that any one of these people could be Celo. He felt he couldn't trust anyone and yet he had the overwhelming urge to stop someone and ask for help. He envied the fact that each of them was going about their normal lives, whilst he carried the burden that there was a mad man somewhere in town threatening to kill his friends. He checked the time on the mobile phone and immediately picked up the pace.

Peter was practically running now as he continued up the road, thoughts racing round in his mind, firing up his synapses like lightning in an electrical storm. The name Celo, why was he using a Latin word? Was there any other significance to it, beyond its basic meaning? A sign that Celo was educated? Or a lame attempt to appear intelligent? Peter figured you could easily find out the Latin word for anything through a quick search via Google. It did suggest that he must be someone Peter knew, or else why the need for an alias and a disguised voice? He'd immediately assumed from the depth of the voice that it was a man, but on further reflection he had no idea how good these devices were so it could just as easily be a woman. He shook his head in frustration; his questions were just throwing up more questions than answers.

As he reached the busy junction at the top of the road, he could see the dilapidated flats looming in the distance. They did seem to be reaching up and touching the sky, as Celo's clue suggested. He stopped at the junction and waited for a gap in the traffic, bending over at the waist to catch his breath. Despite the intense burning in his stomach and face from running he still felt bitterly cold, and his hands were trembling violently. He negotiated his way through the traffic and crossed over the junction onto Plumer Drive, then continued towards the flats.

His first goal had been to simply get to the flats, but as the towering structure grew closer he began to feel more worried. What was he going to do when he actually got there? How was he going to find Colin in that sprawling maze of over a hundred apartments? Celo's clue had indicated something to do with the stairways but Peter doubted that he would be there - surely one of the residents would have discovered him? Colin had to be inside one of the apartments, but which one? He couldn't think of anything in the clue that pointed to a more precise location.

Peter was distracted for a moment as he passed by Bilton primary school. It was the school they'd all gone to as children. The building, the adjoining playground and field used to be open plan but were now surrounded by a foreboding seven foot metal fence. An ugly visual reminder, he thought, of these wary times; as if dangerous people were a new phenomenon. People seemed scared of everything these days, and determined to wrap their children in a cocoon of cotton wool. They seemed to forget that previous generations had negotiated through the same dangers and had emerged relatively unscathed. Peter felt very strongly on the subject and usually reacted with disdain upon reading any news that yet another protective bubble was being created because a so-called professional had theorised that someone might get hurt. However, all of his natural feelings on the subject were confused at present, given his current predicament. The desire to be overprotective seemed to make much more sense with people like Celo in the world. An irony being that this time the adults were the ones who needed protecting.

Peter passed the school and rounded the corner into the cul-de-sac. The flats were built in a dip below street level so at the end of the road was a driveway that spiralled down to the entrance. The grounds surrounding the flats were closed in by a brick wall about eight feet in height, with a steep grass verge leading up to the roadside which was cordoned off with a waist high fence. Peter remembered that when they were younger they used to jump the fence, slide down the grass verge and jump off the edge of the brick wall to land on the ground. As he approached the fence he stopped short, and looked down at the almost vertical drop - age made it look more forbidding.

He ran down by the side of the fence, then down the steep embankment and arrived at the front door to the flats. He tried the door but it was locked. To his right was a keypad and next to that a larger pad with numbers and little slider views next to each. A lot of the apartments looked empty with no names next to them, especially for the 9th and 10th floor. He scoured the list looking for any clue and felt his heart skip a beat when he saw the name C Clark next to Apartment 9 on the 10th floor. He pressed the button and waited anxiously, half expecting Celo's voice to come over the speaker, but nothing happened. He tried pressing the button again but there was no response and the door didn't buzz to allow him entry. For a moment he considered pressing every button on the 1st floor - something they used to do as a childhood dare.

Then he remembered the key with the number nine engraved on it. He pulled the bunch from his jacket pocket and fumbled the correct key into the lock. It slid in easily, he turned the key and the door opened.

Peter went inside and crossed the lobby area, pressing both buttons for the lifts. The one to his left opened straight away and he hurriedly pressed the button for the 10th floor. As the lift noisily and shakily rattled and shuddered its way towards the 10th floor Peter wondered what awaited him. Would Colin be there? Alive, dead? Was Celo there? He wished he had some kind of weapon, and cursed his lack of thought for not grabbing a kitchen knife or something from Colin and Michelle's house. He pulled the mobile phone from his jacket pocket - the time display read 14:51pm.

'Hurry up, hurry up.'

The lift jolted to a stop and pinged to signal its arrival. The doors wobbled opened. Peter stepped out into a corridor lined with doors to each of the apartments. To his left and right were the exits leading to the stairwells. He cautiously crept up the corridor looking for apartment nine. There it was. He put his ear to the door. All was quiet except for the hum of a television coming from one of the other apartments on the floor. He hesitated for a moment wondering whether to knock or just barge in. He leaned in again, and knocked loudly. Immediately he heard a muffled sound. He tried the door handle and found it wasn't locked. He opened the door with his left hand, his right hand clenched tightly into a fist.

CHAPTER 12

14:54pm

Peter had walked directly into the living room of the apartment. And there, silhouetted in front of the main window, was a man strapped into a chair facing the window with his back to Peter. The chair was stood on top of a rectangular black metallic box, which stood about three feet high. The legs of the chair were wedged into grooves running along the top of the contraption like railway tracks, which ran directly towards the window. A large rubber belt was stretched around the back of the chair, hooked to the walls on either side of the window.

As Peter approached the contraption from the right-hand side he could see a thick metal bar standing vertically from the middle of the block. The bar was positioned tightly against the chair between the legs of Colin Clark. The contraption looked like a crude oversized catapult.

On the window itself, a large X had been scored in the glass. Peter had seen enough crime television series to know that this was done to make glass easier to smash.

'Jesus Christ,' he gasped.

Colin could hear him approaching and started shouting in panic, although it was muffled by a black cloth tied around his mouth. He was strapped down like a death row prisoner in the electric chair waiting for the switch to be thrown. Peter could see the heavily bandaged stump where Colin's left arm had been cut off at the elbow joint. There was another strap around Colin's forehead securing it against the head of the chair. His panic-stricken eyes were bulging, struggling to look to his right to see who was stood beside him, and then he recognised him. Peter could hear him saying his name even though it was muffled by the gag in his mouth.

'It's alright Colin, I'm here,' said Peter.

He ducked his head under the thick rubber belt to move closer so he could work on the straps holding Colin to the chair. Peter managed to free his right arm and Colin immediately pulled the cloth from his mouth.

'What the fuck is going on?' Colin screamed as Peter started to work on the buckle strapped to Colin's right leg.

'I don't know. Someone's playing some kind of sick game. Do you remember how you got here?'

'No. I think I was drugged. I just woke up like this. My fucking arm's been cut off Peter!'

'I know. The sick bastard left it in your house to convince me this game was real.'

'What sick bastard? What game?' Colin shouted as Peter managed to free his right leg.

He started to work on the strap around Colin's chest as Colin fumbled with one hand at the strap around his forehead.

'I don't know, but he's taken the others as well. He says me and him are playing Hide and Seek.'

'What?'

Colin paused for a few moments trying to take in what Peter was telling him.

'Have you called the police? Michelle's dad?'

'No,' was Peter's terse response.

He was struggling with the buckle on the strap around Colin's chest. It was bound so tightly he couldn't free enough space to release the prong from the hole of the belt.

'Why not?' Colin shouted as he freed his head.

He started to work on the strap around his left shoulder.

The block started to emit an unsettling buzzing noise.

'What's that?' Colin said.

'I don't know. But we have to hurry,' Peter replied, now struggling more frantically with the strap around Colin's chest.

'Breathe in,' he shouted at Colin.

The buzzing grew louder and louder.

'Hurry.'

Peter strained as the prong finally snapped out of the hole and the strap unravelled. He rushed around to Colin's left-hand side, ducking again under the rubber belt, and started to work on the strap around Colin's left leg.

Colin desperately shouted, 'come on' as he yanked at the buckle around his shoulder.

The noise from the block became a high pitched whine.

And then – as unexpectedly as it had begun - the noise stopped. Peter and Colin froze, looking at each other.

Colin started to speak, 'what the....'

In one swift movement the thick metal bar in the middle of the block snapped down, away from the chair. With no resistance against the rubber belt it pushed the chair forward … down the tracks towards the window. Peter grabbed onto Colin's left leg and was dragged forward as Colin and the chair slammed into the window and went through the glass. Peter managed to get half of his body against the wall and window frame. His right hand gripped Colin's ankle as he started to fall head first from the 10th floor. Peter cried out in pain as his arm stretched and jolted stopping Colin upside down in midair. Colin swung back against the outside wall, holding his hand out to stop his face hitting it. Colin watched as the waterfall of glass bounced off the concrete ground ninety feet below him. He screamed in terror. The weight of the chair hanging upside down started to slip over Colin's torso. The strap around his shoulder slid down his arm and came loose over the stump of his dismembered arm. The slightly loosened strap on his left leg started to unravel itself.

Peter could feel that he was being pulled out of the window by the weight. He struggled to stay inside the apartment, his left hand gripping the wall and his toes pressed against the skirting boards. The tendons in his neck pulsed as he strained to pull Colin up. The chair loosened and fell away from Colin. It plummeted to the ground below and shattered on impact in a noisy echo of broken wood, which rattled and bounced off in multiple directions. Colin let out another scream.

Peter was struggling to hold on. The upper half of his body was almost completely out of the window. The rubber belt, now straight across the window, was pressing against his back. He could feel his left hand losing its clawed grip on the wall. His right hand had almost lost its grip on Colin's left leg and he was mainly holding onto the cuffs of his jeans. Peter grunted between gritted teeth as he mustered all his strength to pull Colin back to safety. But the weight was too great. He lost his grip and was left holding nothing. He grasped at thin air and then watched as Colin fell with a piercing scream - suddenly silenced as his body slammed into the ground. Peter was leaning out of the window, his eyes bulging; his hand still outstretched trying to reach for Colin.

Peter pulled himself up slowly and withdrew inside the apartment. He turned with his back against the wall and slid down it to slump on the floor with his head in his hands. He heard the scream of a woman outside; a resident perhaps who had heard the commotion and looked out to see Colin's mangled body.

He sat there in a timeless trance, his head whirling with shock. The sound of police sirens in the distance woke him and he stood up and looked out of the window. Across the town, through the grey sky, he could see the unmistakeable blue flashing lights making their way from the police station at the bottom of the high street. They'd be here in a few minutes. Peter looked down to see a group of people gathered about halfway between Colin's body and the entrance to the flats. A few of them were looking up and pointed accusatory fingers directly at Peter. He instinctively backed away from the window. The William Tell tune began to play as the mobile phone vibrated in his jacket pocket. He knew it would be Celo, probably ringing to gloat, and he could feel anger start to build up inside him. The caller ID displayed 'Peter Stevenson calling' again and he answered the phone.

CHAPTER 13

15:05pm

'You fucking sick bastard. How could you do this?'

Peter was half expecting Celo to taunt him but beneath the metallic distorted voice he could almost hear an ounce of sympathy.

'Peter, you were *so* close. I almost wish you had saved him. He could be a bit of an idiot sometimes but I did like him.'

Peter shouted back.

'Then why? Why did you do this?'

'All will be revealed in due course. But remember Peter that although Colin is dead you still have the opportunity to save the others. You have to carry on with the game.'

The faces of Laura, Cas, Michelle, Cheryl and Steve flashed through his mind. Although it pained him to admit it he had to carry on with this twisted game.

Celo continued. 'You have to get out of the building now Peter. The police will be here soon. And when they find that a police officer has been killed they're going to be gunning for you.'

Peter felt angry at the suggestion that this was his fault.

'You were the one that put me in this situation. You chose Colin to be first.'

'I know you're upset Peter. I know you're angry with me. You can grieve for Colin later, but you have to get out of the building *now*, before the police arrive. If they catch you, you'll not be able to save the others. Think of the others you can save.'

The phone clicked as Celo hung up.

The sounds of the sirens were creeping closer, drawing Peter's attention to the broken window again.

'I'm so sorry Colin,' he muttered under his breath as he left the room.

He ran up the corridor and frantically started pressing the buttons for the lifts. The digital displays above showed that one was on the 1st floor and the other was on the 2nd floor. He stood there for a few moments but the display didn't change. He decided to abandon the lifts and ran for the door leading to the stairwell. He ran down the stairs, jumping down the last half of each flight, like they had done as children. Each jolt as he landed shuddered up through his body, sending a sickening ache through his stomach. He reached the ground floor and ran through the doorway towards the entrance to the flats. He stopped dead in his tracks, with his hand on the door handle, as he saw the crowd of people gathered just outside. A few turned and looked at him, eying him suspiciously. A woman pointed a finger at him and a heavily built man with a shaved head started to walk towards the door, looking directly at Peter. Peter turned and saw a fire exit at the end of the corridor. He started to run down the corridor and as he approached the fire exit he heard a shout.

'Hey, you! Stop.'

Peter looked behind to see that the man had come through the doorway and was running towards him. Peter pressed the security bar inwards and pushed open the fire exit; there was surprising resistance, no doubt it hadn't been opened in years. He ran out behind the back of the flats and quickly surveyed his surroundings. The only escape route was the spiral driveway at the front of the flats … unless he climbed up the wall surrounding the grounds. He ran towards the eight-foot brick wall. He jumped and grabbed the top but his body slammed against the hard surface, winding him and he fell down. The shout came out again.

'Hey, you.'

Peter turned; the shaven headed man had just come out of the fire escape. Around to the side of the building, some people had come from the front entrance to observe the commotion; a second man started running towards him. He back tracked a few steps and jumped again, straining as he dragged himself up the wall. He clambered up the steep grassy incline on all fours until he reached the top. Without looking back he vaulted the small fence, landing in a field and started to run. On the borders of the field ahead and to the left of him was the Glebe estate; to his right was a stone brick wall surrounding the cemetery at the back of Bilton church.

Peter headed for the wall figuring he could hide in the grounds of the cemetery if he was being followed. A variety of trees and bushes were dotted around the perimeter. There were sufficient breaks in the foliage for him to find a safe passage through and he climbed the wall into the church grounds. He ducked behind the wall and - under cover of a bush - he peered over towards the back of the flats. There was no sign of his pursuers and Peter breathed a sigh of relief. Then he saw a pair of hands gripping the fence and a man emerged over the fence onto the field. There was no sign of the large shaven-headed man and Peter assumed that he'd been unable to climb the wall or the steep grass verge. This man was tall, slender and, again, had close-cropped hair; the type of guy you wouldn't quarrel with, not overbuilt but obviously strong. He swept the horizon, his gaze falling on the church.

The man started to come towards the wall and Peter sank back down in panic. He started to move away from the wall, crouching over as the wall was not high enough for him to run upright. He frantically looked around the grounds for a place to hide. He paused for a second, looking over to the far side of the grounds, recognising the very spot where seven of the Excellent Eight had been gathered for the funeral of Gavin Blair, around 24 hours ago. Now there were six.

He didn't have time to dwell on it; the man would be at the wall soon and would easily spot him scuttling around trying to hide. Peter saw a small break in the wall ahead of him which he thought he might be able to squeeze through to hide on the outside of the wall which surrounded the west side of the church. He scurried over to the gap and squeezed his body through and crouched down.

He was on a small dusty path that followed the wall and then curled off in the opposite direction into an alley. He remembered that the alley separated a row of houses that lay on Plumer Drive ahead of the turnoff he had taken into the cul-de-sac to get to the flats. Peter heard the scraping of rock as the man chasing him climbed into the grounds. Peter pressed his body against the wall and stayed quiet, his heart thumping in his chest as he heard the various rustlings of the man searching the cemetery. The noises grew louder as the man approached his hiding spot. Peter's entire body tensed as he heard the branches of a tree, directly behind the wall where he sat, being brushed aside. Peter clenched his fists waiting to fight back if the man should find him.

CHAPTER 14

15:16pm

Peter breathed a sigh of relief as the rustling noises started to move away from him. He edged cautiously up the wall and risked a glance into the grounds. He could see the man on the far side of the cemetery now, near the spot where Gavin was buried, making his way around towards the front of the church. Peter could hear the sounds of an ambulance whining in the distance behind him.

He got up and ran along the dusty path and down the alleyway, slowing as he reached the street. He cautiously looked out onto the street, just as the ambulance came tearing up the road and turned into the cul-de-sac towards the flats. Peter crossed over the road timidly and walked away from the commotion.

He was heading towards the town green, which lay out in front of the church, but realised that the man who had been chasing him might come back around this way after leaving the church. He decided to turn right and descended a flight of stairs which brought him down into Crooksbarn estate which lay directly behind the primary school he had passed earlier. This was considered 'the posh end of town' and he briskly walked down the street past the large townhouses. He had no idea where he was going and just walked aimlessly, his eyes darting to and fro nervously.

He continued to walk, with hunched shoulders, deeper into the maze of streets within Crooksbarn estate. He lost track of time. Eventually he stopped in the middle of a street. The world was spinning around him, as if he was stood on a merry-go-round. He felt sick, he had to sit down. He perched himself on the edge of a wall. He was shivering uncontrollably. He put his hands to his mouth, the image of Colin plunging from the flats to the ground below played over and over again in his mind like a movie clip on a loop. He retched and started to dry-cough, but he wasn't sick. He spat a little but his mouth was very dry. He continued to sit there, shivering and staring into thin air. A fine mist of rain fell silently.

The William Tell tune snapped him back to life. He held the mobile phone out in front of him staring at his own name flashing up on the screen. He didn't want to answer it. He didn't want to be here. He wanted to be home right now with his wife and son. Why had he come to this godforsaken town again? He hadn't seen Gavin in over twenty years; he shouldn't have come to the funeral.

The phone stopped ringing and immediately he felt guilty. What about the others out there? Probably trapped, alone and afraid, not even aware that they were part of this sick bastard's game. What if Celo didn't ring back? What if he thought that Peter had been captured in the flats? Then the phone started to ring again and this time Peter answered quickly.

'I'm here,' he breathed.

'Congratulations on your escape. It was a little bit close for comfort in the cemetery wasn't it? I thought that guy was going to find you, cowering behind the wall.'

Peter looked around him again and wondered where the killer was. Celo had to have been in the flats, maybe even in the next apartment; he could have watched him from the 10th floor window as he scrambled up the hill, jumped the fence and ran into the cemetery. Or could he have been one of the men giving chase? Pretending to be a concerned citizen? Whatever, this guy seemed to be everywhere. Was Celo watching him right now?

'I know you must be in shock, but you don't have time to mourn.'

Peter interrupted, 'I don't want to do this anymore.'

'Peter, it's far too early in the game to give up. I know you're disappointed that you've lost one but you can come back from this.'

Peter pleaded, trying to appeal to Celo's sense of humanity.

'I know you keep saying this is a game, but it's not. Colin is dead.'

Celo responded, unmoved.

'Exactly, so you have to ask yourself, would you rather be the seeker or one of the hiders? Would you rather be depending on someone else to come and save you? You can be their saviour Peter. The other members of the Excellent Eight need you to be strong right now. We're on a tight timescale and we need to get on with the game.'

Peter found Celo's attempt to console and motivate him disconcerting.

'I just need to rest a bit; I've been running for thirty odd minutes.'

'I know, but you don't have time Peter. Besides the more time you have to think about it, the more you'll become upset about Colin. I'm going to give you the next clue.'

Celo was using the old adage: you have to keep yourself busy after a trauma to avoid the inevitable feelings of grief and sadness. But this was ridiculous; he didn't feel ready for the next clue. However, he couldn't even muster up the strength to argue with Celo, and what use would it do anyway?

Celo gave him the next clue.

'It's a place where you used to go with the boys and the girls. She likes everything that Lawrence's bakes. She'll get fat if she eats all the cakes. Cheryl Stimson probably has good and bad memories of this place. You have until four o'clock to find and save her.'

Peter looked at the time on the phone and saw that it was 15:27pm. He suddenly found his anger.

'33 minutes? That's not long enough. You have to give me more time!'

'Sorry Peter. The times have been set, I can't change them.'

And with this final comment Celo ended the call.

Peter repeated the clue in his head again. He was surprised how obvious it was. He knew exactly where he had to go.

CHAPTER 15

15:27pm

Martin Lawrence's sweet shop stood in a row of four shops on Low Grange around the corner from the secondary school they all attended. They used to sneak out of school at dinner time and go around to Low Grange because there was a chip shop too. The Excellent Eight were not the only children who did this but one time they were all spotted by Mr Morgan who happened to be driving past. In hindsight Peter thought it was silly of them to run because Mr Morgan had seen them all anyway. Sure enough they were called one by one from their classes that same afternoon, down to the head teacher's office to be scolded for going off school grounds during school hours. This had stopped the Excellent Eight from going to the shops for at least a week, which was considered about the right amount of time to stay off Mr Morgan's radar. The task of tolerating proper school dinners for a whole week was punishment enough.

Cheryl Stimson had not always been as thin and attractive as men found her now. When the Excellent Eight were children Cheryl used to eat her fair share of junk food and was an extremely chubby young lady. At Martin Lawrence's sweet shop she would often spend more money than the other seven combined. Most might get a bag of chips for 50p and then a 10p mixed bag of sweets from Martin Lawrence's shop. Cheryl would forego the chip shop and spend all her money in Martin Lawrence's on the numerous sweets and cakes on offer. She would hardly ever have the same thing twice and used to relish the variety that was the cake slice of the day.

Cheryl had not always been as arrogant and stuck-up as she was now. In those days Cheryl was a quiet girl who was generally considered a goody two-shoes. If anything, she was the quietest and shyest member of the Excellent Eight, and the group could probably have been blamed for leading her astray on many occasions; coercing her to do things she wouldn't normally have done. The perils of peer pressure, Peter thought. He reflected on how much she had changed since those childhood days and decided that he had preferred her back then. She used to have a certain warmth to her and he had especially liked the way that she could be depended on to laugh at all his jokes, no matter how lame they were. He had only seen her briefly and swapped small talk pleasantries before Gavin's funeral. Afterwards he had specifically sought her out to catch up and observed that she was a little standoffish and dismissive, batting away his attempts to strike up a conversation. He felt that her warmth had been replaced by a sense of bitterness and resentment, which he felt must have matured over the years as she had lost weight and become more attractive to the opposite sex.

On the day they were all spotted by Mr Morgan, everybody had run off and escaped except Cheryl, who - balancing a crammed and messy éclair - had stood rooted to the spot outside the shop. She was collared by Mr Morgan and dragged back into the school. The whole episode upset her deeply, especially as Mr Morgan told her that her parents would be contacted regarding the incident. Ultimately the head teacher had decided to just warn the children, a decision which was taken badly by Mr Morgan who, Peter believed, relished getting children into as much trouble as possible.

Peter recalled being summoned to the head teacher's office with Cas who was in the same class as him at the time. They had laughed and joked all the way there, it was nothing new for them. Cheryl was in the foyer where she'd been standing for at least two hours. She kept her head down the whole time they were there, as if truly ashamed at what she had done, her face hiding behind her mopped hair. It was clear that she'd been crying. Peter was aware that Cheryl's parents considered her to be their golden girl and put a lot of pressure and high expectations on her to be the best. However, it hadn't occurred to him that Cheryl was upset because she was worried that her parents' impression of her would be tarnished by this incident. Peter and Cas, and the other members of the group, couldn't have cared less because they all knew that even if their parents were contacted they would, at the very most, receive a light scolding - it was such a minor incident. In fact, Peter reckoned that Cas' father would have shouted more at the teachers for bothering him over nothing.

Peter finished his reminiscence and started to walk briskly out of the street. He couldn't remember too much about the layout of Crooksbarn as they didn't often venture here when they were children. He did remember that there was another exit over the far side of the estate that would bring him out onto a main road, Hyde Avenue. He could cross this road to get onto Wolviston estate. He would have to go through Wolviston estate to get onto Low Grange North before heading down into Low Grange South where the school and the shops were. Again, it was a large distance to cover in thirty minutes, and he lamented the fact that it would take about five minutes in a car.

Peter started to pick up the pace, ignoring the aching burning sensation in his shins and feet. The path leaving the estate, even though it was still daylight, was dark; concealed as it was by ten foot high fences and trees either side. About half way down the path he jerked to a stop as he saw a police car race by the exit with its lights flashing. It reminded him that every police officer would be getting drafted in to investigate the death at the flats because it involved one of their own. He felt a slight sense of relief that the police might be preoccupied at the scene, and might not be looking for him yet as they would be interviewing all the residents of the flats. He then felt a surge of guilt at considering the death of his friend Colin as a fortunate distraction for the police. He continued down the path. He was pretty sure no one would have recognised him but enough people had seen him to give the police a general description. He had to be careful, he couldn't get caught or he'd forfeit the game, as Celo had put it.

Peter arrived at the exit to the path and cautiously observed the traffic streaming up and down Hyde Avenue. He timed his runs to the break in the traffic to cross over and into Wolviston estate. He ran as fast as his body would let him, again questions went through his mind as he tried to make some sense out of what was happening. One nagging suspicion was standing strongly at the forefront of his mind. Celo must be a member of the Excellent Eight.

CHAPTER 16

15:39pm

Peter came running out of Wolviston estate, crossing over onto the road that ran through the middle of Low Grange North into Low Grange South. He looked at his mobile whilst running; 21 minutes to go.

Peter continued with his train of thought. Celo had to be a member of the Excellent Eight. How else could he know so much about the group? Maybe he'd gained the information under duress from each person, but it didn't seem likely. Besides, Colin had said that he had just woken up in the flats and didn't mention seeing or speaking to anyone. Colin thought he'd been drugged ... if so, *how* were they drugged? Were they all drugged in the pub, something slow acting that was put in their drinks maybe? Peter tried to recall anything unusual with the drinks bought last night but nothing stood out. Something bugged him, if Celo had drugged them in the pub how would he be certain that they would all get to Colin and Michelle's house before passing out? Celo must have drugged them all back at the house. He tried to remember who was serving the drinks. He could only remember having a couple of bottles before blacking out. He wasn't sure but he thought he could recall Steve handing out bottles to him and Cas. He remembered what he'd considered earlier about a potential affair between Steve and Michelle. What if they were working together? Neither of them had been brought into Celo's twisted game so far.

Peter wondered if he was right about the affair between Steve and Michelle. When they were younger, all the boys knew that Colin fancied Michelle, and they were sure Laura and Cheryl knew how Michelle felt about Colin but the two sexes didn't share their knowledge. Colin always sought attention from Michelle in that silly, childish way boys have of flirting with girls when they have no idea how to flirt. He would goad her and pick on her continuously to drive her crazy enough to give him attention. In response Michelle would look at the other girls, feign upset at Colin's comments, say that she hated him unconvincingly and then usually hit him in the arm. Despite one awkward kiss between them - brought about by peer pressure - they didn't get together when they were younger. Peter had heard from Gavin, a number of years ago, that Colin and Michelle had finally started dating when they were in their mid-twenties and had married six years ago, a few months before Peter had married Janine. For a second, a part of him hoped – almost believed - that this game would only involve Colin and Cheryl. Maybe Steve and Michelle had some motive for killing them both. Peter could form some semblance of a motive towards Colin based on whether he was right about the affair and the father of the unborn child, but he struggled with why Cheryl would be involved.

It was obvious to Peter from last night's party that Steve and Colin were good friends. Although Peter did remember that Colin had gotten irritable on a number of occasions when Steve cracked a derogatory joke about him, but Peter just took that as friendly banter. Michelle and Cheryl were good friends as well. Peter had observed nothing untoward with them, and in fact they had talked and laughed together most of the night; so much so that Peter remembered looking over to Laura who obviously felt out of touch with her two former girlfriends. Peter couldn't recall any ill word or argument taking place between them. But that doesn't mean anything he thought, there could quite easily be other things brooding under the surface, which he didn't know about.

Peter felt like he was clutching at straws and his initial hope started to fade. Why would Celo mention the Excellent Eight so much if this game was only going to involve the death of Colin and Cheryl? And surely Michelle wouldn't be involved in anything like this when expecting a child? The only thing he did know was that he couldn't bring himself to find a disclaimer for Steve yet and he was currently at the top of his list of suspects.

Peter continued down the road, past the small fields either side which separated Low Grange North from Low Grange South. His face felt like it was on fire, and his lungs burned with his heavy panting. The rain had been getting steadily heavier over the last ten minutes but it offered no comfort to cool his burning face. His clothes were wet through and stuck to his body, making his movement more uncomfortable. He pulled out the mobile phone and checked the time; he had just fifteen minutes to save Cheryl.

CHAPTER 17

15:45pm

Peter ran past a man on his driveway washing his car, even though the rain was falling. Such a typical thing to do on a Sunday afternoon, he thought. He wished he was doing the same right now.

He used to go out and wash the car on a Sunday afternoon whilst Janine prepared the dinner. They would usually have Janine's mother Ann over on a Sunday and they'd stand in the kitchen gossiping. Janine would cook, as Ann played with George. He used to leave them to it and go out and wash the car as it gave him some peace and quiet and allowed him to think about the week that had passed and the one to come. He'd then go in for, what was by far, the best meal of the week. Usually at work he'd be lucky if he had time to cram a sandwich down his throat whilst sat at his desk.

After Sunday dinner he'd take over responsibilities for entertaining George as Janine and her mother, who'd usually open a bottle of wine to accompany dinner, would continue drinking and chatting. Ann would stay long enough to see George bathed and put to bed around 8pm and she'd probably last another half an hour before she would start yawning. She would say the same thing every week, which was that she wasn't sleeping well but the wine combined with the large meal, was making her sleepy now. Peter would take the hint and drive her home. The journey normally took fifteen minutes and he would help her into the house, usually carrying in the bags of leftovers that Janine had made up for her and popping them in the freezer. He always felt a little sorry leaving her there on her own. Her husband, Janine's father John, had died five years ago from a stroke. They had been a jovial couple who clearly depended on each other; the kind who finished each other's sentences, an understanding that had come from 45 years of marriage. As if the death of Janine's father wasn't enough, Ann herself had a stroke six months after John's death. Fortunately it had only been a mild one but the left side of her body was partially paralysed and so she needed a walking stick to get around. They would exchange pleasantries and then part company. He would drive home, open a can of lager and cuddle up to Janine on the couch to watch the forgettable programmes that comprised Sunday evening television. Janine would be slightly drunk from the wine so she was often a little frisky and if George was good and stayed in his bed they would normally retire around 10pm to make love.

Peter smiled as he remembered that last weekend she had used sex as a bargaining tool. She had waited until he was horny and vulnerable and then made him promise to take the car to the garage on the Monday morning to have the tyres replaced. He'd promised, and then clearly forgotten, hence why she'd mentioned it again in their phone call yesterday.

Peter wished that he could go back to last Sunday, to mundane tasks like washing his car, before any of this had happened. But this was not a typical Sunday afternoon. He had been removed from his cosy life and forcefully shoved into this twisted game. A game with serious consequences, where people were dying, people he knew.

The happy memories of his lazy Sundays faded away, and the harsh reality of his current situation came sharply back into focus. Running down the road, he could feel every jolt as his legs hit the uneven pavement.

Peter thought back to the contraption that Colin had been rigged up to. It wasn't something you could pick up from a hardware store; and so it must have been created by Celo for this lethal game. Did it give any clue as to who Celo was? He imagined a shady figure silhouetted in black in some basement working on the contraption, continuously testing it to make sure it would carry out its deathly function. Peter couldn't recall any one of the Excellent Eight being particularly good at metalwork at school, and considering their chosen professions in adulthood nothing particularly stood out.

His mind fleeted back to the flats. He wished he'd had more time. Wished he'd been able to ask someone about the apartment where he found Colin. Had any of the neighbours seen anyone going into the apartment? Had Celo rented it under his real name? Maybe the police would be looking into it? They could be looking for him right now. Peter wondered what that would mean, as far as the game was concerned, if the police were to find Celo. If he were caught would the remaining members of the Excellent Eight die? No, Celo wouldn't be so stupid as to rent out an apartment in his own credentials. He'd use somebody else's identification - stolen or fake ID. He wondered to himself whether it was actually possible to fake identification or whether he was simply thinking that because of all the movies he had seen. An immediate worry grew in Peter, Celo had *his* wallet. What if Celo had used his driving licence and credit cards to rent out the apartment? No, it was highly unlikely that Celo could rent it on a Sunday morning, pick up the keys *and* get Colin and that apparatus in. It must have been rented out earlier and Colin was taken there during the night whilst everyone else was sleeping peacefully in their beds unaware that a deranged killer was creeping around the corridors.

Peter ran directly past the road leading down to his old secondary school. As he passed he took a fleeting glance down the road and saw an eight foot high fence surrounding the field, which sloped down to the school. It was another fence which hadn't been there when he was a child. Through the gathering fog he could just make out the outlines of the roofs of the school buildings. Peter rounded the corner towards Low Grange shops, slowing his pace to a stop so he could take in his surroundings.

He looked over to the four shops; the chip shop was still there, although it looked like it was under a different name. There was a charity shop and then a newsagent. All three shops were closed. Finally, what was formerly Michael Lawrence's sweet shop was now a bakery. The four shops stood on an island of pavement in the sea of the residential estate. There was an alleyway at either end leading round the back to a row of garages belonging to some of the houses on the estate. And - at the side of the buildings - a flight of stairs led to a first floor balcony and the doors to the flats above the shops.

Where was Cheryl? Actually in the shop? Or in the flat upstairs? Celo's first clue hadn't been completely specific. It had mentioned the incident with Colin falling down the stairs, but he wasn't on the stairs ... he was in one of the apartments on the top floor. However Celo had left him another clue on the keypad at the entrance to the flats, but what if Peter had missed that clue? He didn't have time for this. He looked at his watch; 11 minutes to go.

Peter ran up to the shop entrance and tried the door. Locked. He retrieved the keys from his jacket pocket and tried all of them, none worked. He cupped his hands to the window and peered in. It was shrouded in darkness, nothing moved, nothing looked out of place.

Peter ran up the stairs to the balcony at the back. He looked out over the garages opposite - behind them was the cricket grounds and club where his father used to take him when he was younger.

Peter approached the door to the flat directly above the bakery. He felt unsure of what to do so he knocked on the door and waited. There was no answer and no movement to suggest anyone was in. The curtains of the adjoining window were drawn so he couldn't look in. Peter tried the door handle. Locked again. He retrieved the keys from his jacket pocket and his trembling hands messily tried the keys once more. He was terrified as to what to expect this time. Would Cheryl be rigged to another contraption like Colin was? This flat wasn't high enough to throw Cheryl out and kill her. Peter took a deep breath and turned the last key, the lock clicked and the door started to swing open of its own accord.

Peter timidly entered the flat. The light from the open doorway cast his silhouette across the entire room. He could see a light switch on the wall beside the door and he flicked it on. It was a small living room with nothing but a couch in the middle of the room. There were no pictures on the walls and no television; it looked like no one had lived here for a while. Peter closed the door behind him and crossed over to the first door and leant his head into the kitchen to look around. It was a very small kitchen with nothing of interest. Peter moved to the next door and opened it; it was a small bathroom with a shower over a bath, a toilet and sink. Peter moved to the next door and found the single bedroom, again with barely enough space to contain the most meagre furnishings. Peter opened the last door to find stairs leading down. The stairwell was dark and he could hardly make out the door at the bottom. He flicked on the light switch and felt an immediate sense of dread upon seeing a message, scrawled in red paint on the door.

The message said, 'Your dinner is in the oven darling.'

CHAPTER 18

15:52pm

Peter climbed down the stairs and tried the door. It was unlocked and opened outwards into the kitchen behind the counter. The shop was cast in an eerie light from the overcast daylight shining in through the large windows at the front of the shop. He could see an orange light reflecting across the black and white tiled floor coming from behind the door he had just come through. He could also hear a humming noise and his nose picked up an unmistakeable burning smell. He turned round the corner to see that the orange light was emanating from the small window of a six foot high industrial oven nestled in the back corner of the shop. He recoiled in shock at the realisation that Cheryl could be in the oven. He ran over to the oven and looked through the small glass panel. His worst suspicions were confirmed. Through the glass viewer he could make out the shoulder of a woman lying on her side, seemingly unconscious, her whole body pressed against the oven door. He tried to open the door but it was jammed and only opened slightly at the top. He noticed a bulky chain was coiled around the handle and secured with a padlock to a metal loop ring on the top of the oven. The sudden movement of the door opening jolted Cheryl awake and she let out a throaty dehydrated cry.

'Help!'

Peter tried to reassure her, 'Cheryl, it's Peter. I'm going to get you out of there.'

Cheryl started to scream, 'Peter, help me,' banging her fists against the inside of the oven door.

Peter could feel the extreme heat leaking out from the small crack at the top of the oven door. He looked around for the controls. He could see a shiny plate of black metal was screwed to the oven and realised it was covering them.

Cheryl shrieked 'Get me out of here!'

He ran around to the side and looked down the small gap behind the oven for the plug. He tried to slide his hand down the back to pull it out but it was beyond his reach. He took a few steps back and ran shoulder first slamming his whole body weight into the oven to try and move it but it was far too heavy. His eyes darted around the shop desperately searching for something that could help him. He ran to the work surface of the counter and started frantically opening the cupboards below it. He found a shovel, used to slide trays onto the oven shelves. He ran back to the side and slid the shovel down the gap trying to negotiate it to hook around the plug cable.

'Come on,' he shouted as the plug teetered agonisingly just out of the socket.

With a final pull the plug came out and the orange light flickered and died out. A few seconds later the humming ceased. Cheryl was still screaming and bashing her fists against the oven door. He ran around to the front of the oven. Cheryl's hand was scrambling out of the opening at the top of the door, pulling at the chain, and he grabbed her hand to try and reassure her. Her hand was swollen and covered in blood, cut open from punching and hitting the oven door from the inside. Cheryl's screams slowly became whimpers. Although the oven was off, Peter could still feel the heat pouring out. With his free hand he yanked furiously at the handle of the oven, bucking back and forth to try and loosen it. His eyes started to well up with tears of frustration. He looked around the shop again and noticed the till register. He broke free of Cheryl's grasp and she immediately cried out.

'Don't leave me.'

'I'm not going to leave you Cheryl.'

He grabbed the till register and lifted it to chest height.

'Cheryl, move away from the door. I'm going to smash it open.'

He didn't wait for a reply, the till was a lot heavier than he expected, and so he quickly strained and lifted it above his head. He ran forward to gain momentum and smashed it into the oven door. The violent contact sent a sickening shudder through his body, but the damage to the oven was minor. There was a small dent in the door, while the glass had cracked slightly in the corner and now looked like a spider's web. The till looked like it had come off worse, but he picked it up again and crashed it down directly onto the handle. Again, he felt the shudder throughout his body. He tried the handle again, yanking it back and forth rapidly.

'Come on you fucking bastard,' he yelled in frustration.

The handle buckled and one side suddenly snapped away from the door, sending Peter sprawling backwards onto the floor. He looked up to see the handle hanging off the oven door and scrambled to his feet. He unravelled the chain and slid it down over the handle before throwing it up onto the roof of the oven.

The oven door opened and Peter was hit in the face by a hot blast of air followed by the smell of charred flesh. It reminded him of being in a sauna when it hurt to breathe in the hot air. Peter grabbed Cheryl who recoiled in pain at the touch. She muttered incomprehensibly as he dragged her body from the oven to rest her on the floor. She was completely naked and her back was black and red, a horrific combination of burnt flesh and blood. The left side of her body, which had been laid on the metal shelf of the oven, was even worse. Large sections of her skin had peeled and torn off when he pulled her from the oven. Peter retched, his face contorted in a mixture of anger and distress.

'Oh God,' he wept.

Cheryl hunched up in the foetal position and sobbed uncontrollably as Peter pulled the mobile from his jacket pocket and dialled 999. A pre-recorded, female voice spoke.

'Sorry, it has not been possible to connect your call.'

'Shit,' he shouted.

He looked at the display on the phone. The graphic showed he had sufficient reception. Peter wondered if Celo had blocked the phone somehow, but even if he had Peter thought you could always still ring the emergency services. He searched for a phone in the shop and found one hung on the wall and dialled again. A female voice answered.

'Which service do you require?'

'Ambulance.'

'What is the address of the emergency?'

'Low Grange, I'm at Low Grange in Bilton, in the bakery.'

The woman paused for a few moments.

'Is that Low Grange Avenue?'

'Yes,' he said impatiently.

'Can you verify the telephone number you're calling from?'

Peter checked the wall unit and the phone itself but there was no number.

'I don't know what the number is.'

'Okay. What is the problem? Tell me exactly what's happened.'

Peter paused for a second trying to think how he was going to explain the situation.

'My friend Cheryl was trapped in an oven. She's got burns all over her body.'

The woman on the other end of the line paused for a few seconds. Peter had no doubt that an emergency call operator had heard all manner of stories over the years but the pause suggested to him that this was a new one for her.

'Are you with Cheryl now?'

'Yes.'

'How old is she?'

'Erm...33 or 34, I'm not sure.'

'Is she conscious?'

He looked down at Cheryl who was still curled up in the foetal position sobbing.

'Yes, she's conscious.'

'Is she breathing?'

'Yes.'

'Is she away from the oven now?'

'Yes, I got her out; she's laid on the floor. What do I do?' he whimpered in frustration.

'What's your name?'

He felt hesitant at first but answered.

'It's Peter.'

'Okay Peter, is any item of clothing burning or smouldering?'

'No, she's not wearing any clothing.'

Again, the operator paused for a few seconds. It seemed like an eternity to Peter.

'Is she wearing any jewellery around the affected areas?'

Peter leant over Cheryl inspecting as best he could.

'No, it doesn't look like it.'

'Okay, Peter an ambulance has been dispatched and will be there shortly.'

The operator hung up. Peter was left holding the phone, amazed at how abruptly the call had ended.

He shouted out a few times, 'Hello?'

The phone buzzed with the dialling tone. As soon as Peter hung the phone back on the wall unit his mobile phone started to ring. The caller ID displayed his name. He knew it was Celo calling again, his anger boiled up.

'Is she done yet?' Celo asked.

'Fuck you. You sick bastard,' Peter shouted.

'Sorry, that was in bad taste. The best way to treat burns is to apply wet towels. I've left you some over by the sink. Soak them in water and apply them to the worst affected areas.'

'Worst affected areas? She's burnt all over her body for God's sake.'

'An ambulance is on the way. So do what you can for her quickly, to ease her suffering, and then get out of there because the police will probably arrive first.'

'You called the police?' Peter asked.

'No, but you tripped a silent alarm when you opened the door to the shop.'

'Listen, you sick fuck. I'm not going anywhere. I'm staying here with her.'

'That wouldn't be very wise. Come on Peter, you're doing well. After the initial hiccup with Colin you're starting to get into your stride. Sure, Cheryl won't ever be so pretty again, but she *is* alive. You saved her. Now just think of the others you can save. Cas, Steve, Michelle, and of course, Laura. I reckon you have a couple of minutes before the police arrive to think about it.'

Celo hung up and Peter scrunched up his face in anger, tempted to smash the mobile phone against the wall. The sound of Cheryl whimpering brought him back into the moment. He looked around the kitchen and saw the towels rolled up next to the sink. Peter grabbed them and threw them into the sink dowsing them in water from the tap. He scooped them from the sink and, crouching on one knee, started to delicately apply the towels to Cheryl's burnt skin. Celo's words were playing over in his mind. He felt terrible and extremely guilty at what he had thought earlier about Cheryl and her good looks, and cursed himself for thinking along the same lines as the psycho Celo. He wanted to stay here and make sure that Cheryl was alright especially because he feared that if he left her she could still die from shock. However, his mind pictured his remaining friends. He saw the grin of his best childhood friend Cas as they play fought each other. He remembered trading stickers in the playground with Steve who always managed to get the rare ones. He thought of Michelle sucking on her asthma inhaler after laughing too hard. He pictured the shy, beautiful smile of his childhood sweetheart Laura. Peter placed the last few remaining towels on Cheryl and looked at her apologetically.

'I'm sorry Cheryl, I have to go.'

Cheryl's eyes opened, she sat bolt upright and her hands grabbed Peter's arm. He was startled and had to wrestle himself free as he stumbled back onto his rear and shimmied away. Cheryl's outstretched arms grasped for him before returning to cuddling herself as she continued to sob. Peter stood up and turned towards the front of the shop looking out of the window.

'The ambulance will be here soon Cheryl. You're going to be alright.'

He was suddenly blinded by the flashing lights of a police car as it screeched to a halt in front of the shop.

CHAPTER 19

16:06pm

Peter turned and ran back through the kitchen sidestepping Cheryl and ran up the stairs to the flat above. He ran through the living room and out the open door onto the balcony. In the short time he had been inside the shop the early dark nights had already started to creep in. The rain had stopped for now, but the winds continued to whistle.

He crept along to the edge and peered around the corner, wondering whether to risk going back down the stairs. He didn't have to ponder much longer as a policeman appeared at the bottom, blocking his exit. He caught sight of Peter and shouted out.

'Police!'

Peter turned and ran back along the balcony. He clambered over to the other side of the wet metal barrier with his toes teetering on the edge. He crouched down and started to climb down the outside of the building; his feet hanging off into nothing. The policeman reached the top of the stairs and shouted again.

'Stop, police!' as he ran towards Peter.

Peter hung from the ledge and dropped down as the policeman leant over the bars to grab him. He fell ten feet and landed heavily on the gravel of the alleyway, the momentum of his drop making him stumble and fall backwards to the ground. The policeman shouted out for his colleague.

'Mike, he's in the alleyway.'

Peter clambered to his feet, looking left and right wondering which way to go. The policeman on the balcony, deciding not to risk a similar jump, turned and ran back towards the stairs. Peter heard him shout again to his colleague who he assumed was at the foot of the stairway.

'Go round the other side.'

Peter realised he couldn't escape from the alley. He turned and ran towards one of the garages and jumped up to grab the roof. He hadn't done anything like this since he was a child but was surprised how easily it came back to him. He pulled himself up with his fingers whilst using his feet to scramble up the front of the garage door. He got his upper body above the roof line and slumped onto the top of the garage and shuffled the rest of his lower body onto the roof. The two policemen ran into the alleyway from opposite sides of the buildings and ran towards him. He stood up and started to step gingerly over the ivy covered felted roof, almost tiptoeing, worried that at any moment it would crack and break and he would crash through into the garage below. He made it to the other side and jumped down onto a patch of unkempt grass and ran over the uneven surface. He fought his way through the thin tree saplings sprouting from the ground until he reached the wire fence surrounding the cricket pitch. As he vaulted over the fence he took a chance to look behind him. He could see that the other policeman, the one called Mike, had just jumped down off the garage roof onto the grass behind him.

Peter sprinted across the middle of the cricket pitch, his feet squelching on the sodden grass. He could hear the sound of an ambulance in the distance and felt a sense of relief that it was most likely heading towards Cheryl. He ran to the side of the cricket stands - down the road between the stands and the car park - and continued down the sloping tarmac drive.

He came out onto Regal Road, a long thin street with terraced houses to the right of him. Down the road to his left was a railway crossing, the track running by the side of the cricket ground. Beyond the railway crossing Peter recalled there was a steep hill leading down to mainly derelict ground which also housed the Marshalls site. It was a merchant's yard for creating and distributing paving slabs, bricks and tiles. On the opposite side of the road were a number of small disused warehouses which covered the ground from the railway crossing up to the alleyway before the terraced houses began. He wondered if he should try and hide within the warehouses.

Peter looked behind him and could see that Mike had just entered the drive and was heading towards him. He realised that the policeman, although tall and slim, couldn't be a fast runner because he'd dropped further behind whilst crossing the cricket pitch. He just had to keep running, Peter thought to himself. He crossed the road and ran down the alleyway behind the terraced houses. At the end of the alleyway there was a junction where he could either turn back out onto Regal Road or take a cycle path which led down to Sudbury Lane. The lane had approximately twenty generously-sized houses either side of an extreme decline where the Excellent Eight used to play on their skateboards when they were younger. As he ran down the alleyway towards the junction he could feel his shins throbbing as his feet thumped clumsily on the cobbled floor of the alley. He was panting very heavily, his brow lined with sweat and he had a stitch that ached every time he gasped for breath. He reached the junction and glanced back down the alleyway. He could hear the sound of boots echoing on the cobbles but Mike hadn't rounded the corner yet.

Peter turned and ran down the steep incline of the cycle path. The path was shielded on either side by high wooden fences. As far as he could remember, behind the fence to his left was a wasteland of trees and bushes. Behind the fence to his right was the extended garden of the first house at the top of Sudbury Lane. He managed to bring himself to a stop against a lamppost at the exit of the path and looked down the lane. He tried to remember the layout of the streets that led from the junction at the bottom of the road. To the right the road led into another wasteland which the Excellent Eight had affectionately dubbed 'the tip' as people used it as a dumping ground. The road to the left led through more housing estates. He couldn't think of any viable place to hide and besides every part of his body was aching and he needed to rest. He climbed over the waist high wall surrounding the house and moved into the garden which sloped up the bank beside the cycle path, cut off from view by the high fence. There was a shed at the top of the garden and he ran up behind it and crouched down. Peter froze as he heard the sound of shoes scraping to a stop at the junction of the alleyway on the other side of the fence, inches away from him. He searched for a crack in the fence but it was made of solid timber panels. He could hear Mike panting as he spoke into his radio.

'Adam, I'm in the alley behind Regal Road.'

He paused for another breath.

'I think I might have lost him.'

Peter felt a sense of relief wash over him but knew he wasn't completely safe yet. Mike started to move down the cycle path and passed the spot where he was hiding on the other side of the fence.

'I'm heading down onto Sudbury Lane.'

Peter hoped that he wouldn't look for him in the garden. He figured that Mike would know he could have gained enough distance from him to make it to the junction at the bottom of the road and take either turning. He crouched on his knees behind the garden shed waiting. He attempted to take advantage of the brief respite to regulate his breathing which he had been holding in when Mike was on the other side of the fence. His knees were hurting and he felt slightly wobbly. He clumsily fell back onto his backside, wincing as his feet scraped out noisily across the pavement slab. He sat there waiting. The sound of his own heartbeat drumming in his ears.

Peter crawled up to the edge of the garden shed and timidly peeked around; there was no sign of the policeman. He climbed up onto his feet and looked around again. From his vantage point he had a good view of the houses and half of the road on the right-hand side of Sudbury Lane. He tensed as Mike walked into his eye line at the bottom of the junction. The police officer looked up and down the road and then disappeared down the right turning towards 'the tip'. Peter breathed a sigh of relief.

He crept cautiously back down the garden, keeping an eye on the bottom of the road in case Mike decided to abandon his search and come back to Sudbury Lane. He shuffled backside first over the waist high wall and climbed back up the cycle path to the alleyway junction and took the other route back out onto Regal Road. As he came out of the alleyway, he looked around him and a bolt of fear flashed through him as he saw a police car navigating up Regal Road towards him.

'Shit.'

He immediately back stepped into the alleyway and turned to run back down it. For a second he hoped that he hadn't been spotted but his heart sank as he heard the sound of the sirens blare out.

CHAPTER 20

16:18pm

The police car turned into the alleyway as Peter reached the junction again. He knew he couldn't risk going down the cycle path a second time - he could run into Mike coming back from 'the tip'. He turned and ran round the corner back down the alleyway behind the terraced houses as he heard the tyres of the car scrape across the cobbles as it throttled down the alley. The car screeched to a halt at the junction because the turning was too tight to get the car around the corner. As Peter sped down the alleyway he heard the slam of the car door as the policeman Adam gave chase. He shouted into his radio to his colleague.

'He's in the alley behind Regal Road. I'm pursuing on foot.'

Peter rounded the corner and came back onto Regal Road opposite the cricket club again. For a second he debated whether to go back through into the cricket club and run the exact same way he had come but he didn't know how to get back up onto the garage. Besides there might be more police at the shops attending to Cheryl, he thought. Peter glanced down the road and saw the outline of the Marshalls site, another childhood playground. He started running down the street and passed over the railway crossing and ran unsteadily across the muddy path leading to Marshalls.

Peter got to the entrance to Marshalls and was both surprised and grateful that security hadn't been increased in the twenty years since he'd last been there. Despite the ten foot high perimeter fences, the entrance to the site simply consisted of a barrier fence. Peter vaulted over the fence like a hurdler and continued into the site, which was deserted because it was a Sunday. Peter had chosen to come in here because he was confident he could lose the police amongst the maze of bricks and pavement slabs in the grounds at the rear of the site. There were so many nooks, crannies, crevices and niches to hide in which is why it had been such a brilliant place to play Hide and Seek when the Excellent Eight were younger. Now he was 34 years old and playing Hide and Seek again.

He ran between two industrial warehouses, where the paving slabs, bricks and tiles were manufactured, and into a field of stone pillars. On the left-hand side of the grounds were bricks stacked ten feet high on pallets ready to be shipped off when ordered. The right-hand side of the grounds had paving slabs stacked on pallets. His plan was to do exactly what the Excellent Eight used to do when they were occasionally caught playing in the site by the security guard. He ran down the main path, splashing through the puddles and veered off. He darted between the blocks in a zigzag fashion, moving stealthily as if he was a child again. He continued - deeper into the grounds - until he came to the back row of the brick pillars which towered over him like statues. The last row was only a couple of feet away from the security fence at the back of the site. He could hear the commotion of the policemen entering the site, Mike who had gone towards 'the tip' must have caught up with his colleague Adam. It wouldn't be long until more police arrived, Peter thought.

The pillar of bricks he was stood by had four sets of pavement slabs sat on a square pallet at three different levels like a stairway. One set of paving slabs stopped at about five foot, the second set at about seven foot and the front two sets at about ten foot high shielding him from view. He climbed up the first two steps, crouching behind the two higher sets of paving slabs in front of him and peeked over to see where the policemen were. They were walking down the main path in the middle of the site, each of them looking up and down their respective rows as they passed them by. They were talking to each other. Peter couldn't hear what they were saying but it was obvious they were debating how best to find him. They stopped about half way into the site and after a brief discussion Mike nodded in agreement and turned and ran briskly towards the site entrance. Peter realised that they probably thought they had him trapped in here and Mike was returning to the entrance to make sure he couldn't get past them and leave the site. Adam stood for a few seconds, clearly deciding which row to investigate and then headed away from Peter over to the other side disappearing behind the pallets of bricks.

Peter took the opportunity to stand up. He turned around to the fence, shuffled his feet on the spot to ready himself and then took a short run and jumped over the security fence, pulling his feet up to ensure he didn't catch himself on the spikes. The ground on the other side of the fence sloped down towards the railway line. As Peter's feet hit the ground on the side of the muddy hill his momentum carried him forward. With his arms flailing he tumbled head first, rolling for a few feet before he came to a violent stop at the foot of the hill.

He lay there dazed for a few seconds, not wanting to move in case he had damaged something. He tensed his body in expectation of a sudden onset of sharp pain but apart from a dull aching sensation in his feet he felt okay. He stretched his back as he sat up. He looked back up the hill. It was a more difficult jump than he remembered. He got up and brushed the smeared mud from his knees and backside. He kept an eye on the fence of the Marshalls site as he moved away and crossed back over the railway line. He pushed his way through the bushes at the side of the line and climbed over a rickety fence. He clambered down a small grass hill to reach the road that led to the derelict warehouses behind him. He jogged away from the warehouses, making sure he kept under cover of the trees and bushes by the side of the railway line. Peter continued over into Beckbank estate and only then did he feel safe enough to slow down to a walk.

His hands were stinging slightly and as he turned them over to investigate he saw they were covered in dry blood, with a few spots of fresh blood on top. For a moment he thought all the blood belonged to him, but then realised it was mainly Cheryl's blood that he had on his hands. His stomach shuddered and he began to retch as the images of Cheryl's body, her skin blistered and cracked, flashed through his mind. The day's events overwhelmed him. He couldn't control himself for shivering and crying. Tears started to pour from his eyes, as he hugged himself and wept, rocking on the spot. Peter had never been someone who cried very often. In fact the last time he remembered truly crying from pain was when he was a child and hurt himself playing a game in Durden Woods. He had fallen into a hole and hurt his leg. He had cried then. He hugged himself hard trying to control the feelings washing through him.

He thought back to the time when Janine had been inconsolable after the death of her father. Janine was a strong woman who, like him, didn't cry often and he remembered how helpless and small she had looked, curled up on the bed hugging the quilt which spilled out above her arms and covered her face. He had comforted her during those times the only way he knew how. He did not know what he could say to make the pain go away and all he could do was be there for her and be her blanket. He had held her close as she gripped onto him tightly, shuddering as the waves of emotions flew repeatedly through her body. They stayed there on the bed for hours at a time for a number of days, hardly saying any words. Peter wished that she was here now, to hold him in his hour of need. But she felt very far away, and that only made him cry more.

Peter sat on the wall of a house on the desolate street for more than five minutes as images of Colin and Cheryl flashed through his mind. Eventually, his crying subsided, until he was left shivering, his tear ducts exhausted like reservoirs emptied. He looked up to the grey sky and closed his eyes, inhaling and exhaling deeply to calm himself.

CHAPTER 21

16:34pm

Now the adrenaline from the chase was starting to wear off he could feel all manner of aches and pains, particularly in his legs. His shins felt like someone had beaten them with a crowbar. He felt a cold sensation running down his legs, like tiny drops of blood trickling beneath his skin. To distract himself, he focused again on the twisted game that he knew was set to continue. His foray through the Marshalls site had reminded him of playing Hide and Seek as a child - why was Celo playing Hide and Seek? Did something happen to one of them whilst playing the game? Anything that could suggest a motive for why Celo was doing this?

The two main places they played Hide and Seek were the Marshalls site and Durden Woods. On one occasion he'd hurt his leg in Durden Woods during a game of Hide and Seek. He was the seeker and whilst he was counting to a hundred the others went home and left him searching for them in the woods. He remembered that pretty much all of them had been a victim of that prank at some point. In both Marshalls and Durden Woods the group would often run off and leave the seeker unless the seeker was one of the girls. The boys felt an instinctive protectiveness towards them and never played that prank on them. As he'd searched the woods in vain he'd fallen into a concealed hole and hurt his leg. He was trapped there for a few hours until he was found by a man who helped him out of the hole and returned him home to his worried mother. He'd needed a plaster cast and had missed the last few weeks of the summer holidays and the first month of the new term.

Peter couldn't remember any other significant incidents that occurred in Durden Woods, but he recalled that they were caught playing at the Marshalls site a number of times. They had always escaped in the same way he'd just evaded the police. However, on one occasion, they'd been too slow. Cas, as always the strong protector of the group, was last as he waited for everyone else to jump over the fence. As a result he was caught by the security guard, a large man with a flat head and furry moustache, who had grabbed him by his neck and dragged him back to the main office at the front of the site. The other members of the Excellent Eight circled back around to the entrance making sure they stayed at a safe distance. On a number of occasions Gavin and Peter crept up towards the site to try and get close enough to the reception to catch a glimpse of Cas and find out what was happening to him. However, they'd been spotted on each occasion and chased away. About two hours later, they recognised Cas' father's car pulling up and a sombre young man, with his shoulders slumped and his head down, was escorted out by his father and bundled into the back of the car.

Cas was grounded for three weeks and Peter went around to his house every day to spend a few hours playing games in his bedroom. His father had initially turned Peter away for the first three days of Cas' grounding but eventually let him in on the fourth day. On speaking to Cas, Peter found out that his father was mainly annoyed at him because he had been summoned from his work at the mill and as a consequence had lost a day's pay. There had always been a shortage of money within Peter's own family, but Cas' family had it worse. Cas' mother had a rare debilitating disease which left her practically housebound. She got a pittance in incapacity benefit, which came nowhere near covering the medical bills required to help her. Cas' father worked at the mill, but due to the large number of people requiring work he was lucky to receive a week's worth of work during any given month - the loss of a day's pay was a big deal.

Peter was under no illusion that his father sometimes took out his frustration on the young Cas. Hence it had come as no surprise to Peter when Gavin had informed him that Cas had left the town to work in Manchester as soon as he turned eighteen. It had surprised Peter that, despite her debilitating disease, Cas' mother had outlived his father. He died of a heart attack a few years after Cas moved away. He was only 43. Cas' mother had got steadily worse over the years and shortly after Cas' father died she had been placed in a nursing home on the west side of Bilton where she lived the remainder of her years until her death around four years ago. Suffice to say that neither of his parents had managed to enjoy the benefits of Cas' successful career as the owner of his own accountancy firm. Peter remembered receiving the news from Gavin and had felt the urge to speak to Cas. However, he'd lost touch with his best friend after leaving Bilton himself. He knew that Cas was just a phone call away and that they would easily pick up where they had left off. However, he kept putting it off, until eventually too much time had passed and contacting him seemed somehow awkward and inappropriate.

Peter wondered if Cas could be behind this. Could the time he got caught playing Hide and Seek in Marshalls have somehow been the catalyst for this horrible game? Is this why Peter was the seeker? Because he was his best friend and he felt like Peter had abandoned him when he moved away? Cas had a hard upbringing, but Peter didn't feel hugely sympathetic - so had a lot of people in the town. Could the death of his parents have affected him more than he or anyone else knew? When Peter talked to Cas last night, after the funeral, he had seemed like a man at ease. He seemed especially relieved that his mother was now at peace after many years of slowly losing the battle against her illness. Peter had sensed that there wasn't much love lost with his father, and appreciated that over the years the authoritarian stance of his father had led to some resentment and bitterness. But who didn't have parent issues? Peter himself had issues with his own father and the lack of love he had shown him. He had even discussed this with Cas - telling him that he'd vowed to be the polar opposite with his own son, George. As far as he knew, Cas hadn't been to Bilton since the funeral of his mother four years ago. How could he have set all this up in one day? Renting out apartments and building strange devices that catapult people out of windows? Then again, he had no idea whether Cas had been here since. Maybe he had been secretly visiting the town on frequent occasions to set up this cruel game.

Peter looked at the display on the mobile phone, it had just gone half past four. For the first time, he realised that he'd missed his train. Instead he was stuck here, stranded in this isolated little town like a mouse being batted back and forth by Celo's claws. The other two clues had been set with time limits on the hour and Peter was worried that it was less than thirty minutes to 5pm. He didn't want to play this game but he felt impatient, waiting for the next clue as the minutes ticked away. As if reading his thoughts the muffled sound of the William Tell tune rumbled in his coat pocket. He pulled the phone out and felt an awkward sense of relief to see the caller ID display his name again signalling that Celo was contacting him. He answered the phone.

CHAPTER 22

16:37pm

'Have you managed to rest and recover a little?' The metallic voice rang out with an unnervingly genuine tone.

Peter was still thinking of Cas and his potential involvement in this game. He didn't answer Celo, but jumped in with his own question.

'Why are we playing Hide and Seek? Of all the games we played when we were kids, why Hide and Seek specifically? Does it have some relevance to why you're doing this?'

'Of course it does, Peter. Haven't you remembered what happened yet?'

'I remember Cas being caught in Marshalls by the security guard and being grounded for three weeks. Is that why you had me running through Marshalls?'

'That wasn't my doing. *You* chose to go through there. If you'd listened to me - and got out of the shop before the police arrived - then you wouldn't have gone through that worrying chase. You might easily have been caught.'

Celo was right. He could have taken any number of routes to escape the police. Peter paused for a second and then challenged him.

'Cas? This is you, isn't it?'

'No, I'm not Cas. But then again, I would say that whether I was Cas or not wouldn't I?'

'Look, whoever you are, can't we just talk about it? We don't have to play this game.'

'Peter, it is one of those affairs that cannot be mended by talking. I could have just killed them without going through all this. I asked you before; would you rather be the seeker who has this gift - this opportunity -

to save the people you care about? Or would you rather just be another one of the helpless who can't do anything but sit and hope that they are saved?'

Too many questions flooded Peter's mind and he struggled to make any coherent sense out of them. How could Celo see this horrific game as a gift and an opportunity? Why had Celo made him the seeker? One thought made itself prominent above all the others.

'You're insane.'

'We all go a little mad sometimes. Haven't you?'

Peter felt frustrated.

'You're just being cryptic and talking in riddles.'

'Talking of riddles, it's time for your next clue.'

Before Peter had a chance to retort, Celo continued.

'It's a place where you used to go with the boys and the girls. After the football you went on for a chase. Things will erupt when you're caught stealing in this place. Michelle Heron has bad memories of it. You have till 5:30pm to find and save her.'

Peter was surprised by the change in timing. He was getting more time. He repeated, '5:30pm?'

'Yes, I thought you might need a little extra time for this round.'

Peter felt like he was pushing his luck but asked anyway.

'But you refused to amend the times for Cheryl? If you'd given me half an hour more for her, she wouldn't have been so badly burnt.'

'Just be thankful that you saved her at all. She's alive because of you Peter. I told you, the times have been set, I can't change them. But I did figure that you would need a little break after the last one. You're doing a lot of running around.'

Peter couldn't believe he was going to ask this question but it came out of his mouth before he could stop it.

'Is this another game like Cheryl's or is it like Colin's?'

Celo knew what he was implying.

'This is like Colin's. As long as you get there and you can free her before 5:30pm Michelle and her unborn baby will be completely unharmed.'

Peter felt like a child when he asked pitifully, 'Do you promise?'

'I promise. I swear on both of our lives.'

The phone clicked off.

Peter replayed the clue over in his head and after a few seconds of flipping through the filing cabinet of childhood memories, he found the correct one and knew exactly where to go. He had to get to the high street.

He rose from the wall like a geriatric man from a chair. His legs felt wobbly and the sudden movement made him slightly dizzy. He put his hands on his hips, taking in a few large breaths.

Peter started to wonder why Celo gave him clues at all. If he was honest with himself the clues had been relatively easy for him to recall so far. Why didn't Celo just tell him the name of the person and the place to go? Was there something more significant in making Peter recall the actual incidents from their youth? Or was it just simply Celo's twisted idea of fun?

Peter started walking. He had to choose his route carefully. By now he surmised that the police would have a pretty good idea of who they were looking for; there had been plenty of witnesses who had seen him at both crime scenes. Peter had to assume the police could make a positive ID. Were they only looking for him or could they be on Celo's trail as well? He wondered if that was why Celo had made him the seeker, whether he held some grudge against him, so was framing him for these murders. He was under no illusion that he was likely to be the main suspect for the heinous crimes that had occurred so far. He would have to cross that bridge when he came to it. For now he had to concentrate on getting to Michelle and saving her. He knew a number of back roads and quiet streets he could take to get to the high street but it was still going to be tricky, the police station lay at the bottom of the high street and it was likely to be teeming with agitated policemen, all keen to catch the killer of their colleague, Colin Clark.

Yet he felt surprisingly calm as he started towards the high street, walking briskly rather than running. Not that he thought he could run anymore, he needed more time to recuperate, but the extra time given to him by Celo allowed him a comfortable period to get there, even whilst being cautious. He wondered why Celo had given him extra time on this round. Was it really because he knew Peter would be exhausted from close to two hours of running non-stop? Or was there some other reason?

He went back to his earlier thoughts on whether Steve and Michelle were behind this game. He hated himself for thinking it but knew he had to in order to try and make some sense of all this, and hopefully so he could get one step ahead of Celo, and therefore one step closer to finding out who he was. Peter wondered if he had been given the extra time because they wanted to make sure that Peter saved Michelle and her unborn baby. Maybe they had put Michelle into the game as some attempt to throw Peter off their scent. But it was risky, what if he didn't get there in time? He wondered if it could just be Steve involved in this. A thought crossed his mind which was so obvious he wondered why he hadn't considered it before. He was still convinced that one of the Excellent Eight must be involved, Celo knew too much about them as children. He had therefore assumed that if two people were involved that they must both be members of the Excellent Eight, but he now realised that didn't necessarily have to be the case. It could be a member of the Excellent Eight and somebody else, totally unconnected, someone who was a doctor maybe. It had been bugging Peter that Celo must be associated with the medical profession. Whoever was playing this game had to have some medical knowledge, enough to be able to amputate Colin's arm and then cauterise the wound. Celo also knew how to treat burns victims, like Cheryl. Also someone had to have access to the drugs that they were given last night and enough knowledge to know those drugs would keep everyone unconscious long enough for them to set their wicked plan in motion. Peter felt an anxious worry build in his stomach. He knew that Cheryl would be at the hospital by now. What if Celo's partner in crime was there and decided to finish off the job? He wondered if Celo was playing the game fairly. Peter remembered that he did just say that he could have simply killed them without going through all this. Would he really let any of the Excellent Eight survive even if Peter saved them? Or had he decided that they should all die no matter what the outcome of the game? However, if he had simply wanted them all dead, and to frame Peter for the murders, he could have just killed them all in Colin and Michelle's house last night after they were all drugged. Why go through this convoluted game? Maybe it was a cruel ruse to give them false hope, he thought.

Peter was convinced that Celo must hold some grudge against him. Otherwise he would likely have been one of the members tied up somewhere right now, rigged to some device or contraption, counting down the minutes until something horrific happened to him. But why? Why him? What had he done to upset anyone? Gavin and Colin were dead, Cheryl couldn't possibly be involved. If she was involved then she had paid a high price for throwing him off the trail. That left Steve, Michelle, Cas, Laura and maybe an unknown person. Maybe The Sheriff? He'd considered the first three, but up to now Laura hadn't really crossed his mind. It couldn't be Laura. Even as he thought it, he physically shook his head, as if shaking the thought from his mind.

CHAPTER 23

16:42pm

Peter thought back to Cheryl again. What could he do to make sure she was safe? He wished he could contact Celo, or that Celo would ring again so he could ask him whether Cheryl would be safe. Despite the circumstances, Celo had seemed oddly reasonable and genuine at times, very different to the clichéd cackling, cold-hearted murderers he had seen in so many movies and read in so many novels. How could he get in touch with the hospital? Peter thought again about his current situation and cursed the fact that he had no money. He couldn't ring from the mobile phone because Celo had blocked it somehow. Peter wondered if he could get through to the hospital via a phone box. He knew calls to 999 were free but could he be connected to a hospital for free? If he managed to get through would they even speak to him or tell him anything about Cheryl? He wondered if the police might have placed a security guard outside her room to protect her in case the murderer came back, or whether that was just something he had seen in the movies. Another dreadful thought entered his mind. This all might be a moot point; she was badly burnt over the majority of her body, she may have died from shock. Maybe the one person he thought he had saved hadn't been saved at all. He had to find out if Cheryl was okay.

He had the notion to knock on one of the doors he passed and ask if he could use the phone. He could partly tell the truth: he really had lost his phone and wallet, and he needed to check if a friend was okay. Maybe he could even convince someone to give him a lift to the high street? He stopped and looked around. Was there anyone who he knew living nearby? A parent, a brother or sister of one of the Excellent Eight? He couldn't think of anyone close enough, but dismissed the thought anyway. A parent or sibling might be aware of what was going on and give him up to the police.

Peter decided it had to be a stranger. The more he thought about it, the better the idea seemed. Yet a slight doubt crept into his mind. Would this go against Celo's 'rules'? He tried to remember the exact words that Celo had used, but couldn't. He could only recall that Celo said he wasn't to involve anyone else in the game or it would be classed as an immediate default. If he didn't tell the stranger then surely he wasn't breaking the rules because he wasn't involving them? Again, Peter felt the need to talk to Celo, to clarify the rules.

Ahead of him, a car pulled into the driveway of a semi detached house painted pristine white. Peter watched as a man and woman, who he assumed were husband and wife, got out of the vehicle. The tall slender woman moved towards the front door, opened it and went inside. The short stocky man moved to the back of the car and, opening the boot, started to unload as many bags as possible so he could make the least amount of trips. He managed to grab six heavy looking carrier bags and trotted - hunched over - into the house.

Peter walked briskly towards the house, going over the story he would tell them in his head. He moved the mobile phone from the outer pocket of his jacket to an inside pocket against his chest and picked up the pace, mimicking the run of someone who is desperate. As he got to the driveway, the man was gathering more carrier bags - leaning into the deep boot of the Volvo like a magician placing his head in a lion's mouth. The man heard Peter approaching and instinctively withdrew, and straightened up. Peter spoke first and put on his most humble, nervous sounding voice.

'Hi, I'm really sorry to bother you but I was wondering if you could help me.'

The man looked him up and down, surveying him cautiously.

'What's wrong?'

'I've just heard that a friend of mine has been taken into hospital.'

'I'm sorry,' the man replied courteously.

Peter continued, 'I've lost my phone. I was wondering if you had a phone I could use to ring and see if she is alright.'

The man shuffled on the spot but responded warmly.

'Sure, just a second.'

He closed the boot and walked towards his house. He obviously didn't trust him and maybe thought he was going to run off with his shopping hence why he had closed the boot of the car. But Peter reasoned that was understandable given the situation. The man leaned in through the front door and grabbed his jacket from a peg on the wall. He rummaged through the jacket pockets as he walked back towards Peter and pulled out a mobile phone.

'Here you go.'

He handed the phone to Peter but stood extremely close. For a second, the idea of making a run for it did cross Peter's mind - a working mobile phone would be a great help. However, he didn't want to add petty theft to his list of possible crimes and, exhausted as he was, there was little chance such a manoeuvre would succeed. This guy looked in good shape. His arms looked like bodybuilders and his defined chest muscles could be seen through his tight t-shirt. Peter surmised that this man could easily catch him if he ran, and he would probably give him an extreme beating as well.

Peter smiled, 'Thank you.'

He was unsure of how to contact the hospital.

'I've never had to ring a hospital before. Do you know if you phone 999 or is there a local number?'

The man took the phone back off him and started tapping on the touch screen. Peter noticed the man's wife milling around the entrance to the living room and she cautiously peered out and then walked into the hallway to stand at the door. Peter smiled shyly.

'Hi.'

She smiled back courteously and looked at her husband.

'Martin, what's wrong?'

Without looking up from the phone he said, 'I'm just helping this man.'

He glanced up at Peter with a prompting expression.

'Sorry, Peter, my name's Peter,' he dutifully replied.

Martin continued, 'One of Peter's friends is in hospital. He's lost his phone so I'm trying to find a number to ring them.'

He paused and tilted the phone towards the sky as people do when they think that will help them get a signal.

'Come on,' he whispered impatiently. 'There we go,' he said as he tapped one last time on the touch screen before handing it back to Peter. 'It's ringing.'

Peter waited as the ringtone hummed in his ear before the crackle of someone picking up. He heard the weary voice of a woman who was obviously near the end of a long shift.

'Bilton General Hospital. How may I help?'

Peter knew that they wouldn't give out any information if he said he was a friend so he lied.

'Hello, I'm trying to find out about my sister, Cheryl Stimson.'

'Please hold whilst I transfer you.'

Peter held on and looked up at Martin.

'They're just transferring me.'

He realised that Martin was looking at him strangely. The difference between Peter saying Cheryl was a friend and then saying she was his sister was obviously going through his mind. Another woman came onto the phone, sounding even wearier than the last.

'Hello, Burns Department.'

'Hello, I'm enquiring about a woman that's just been brought in, Cheryl Stimson.'

'Are you a relative?'

'Yes, I'm her brother Peter.'

Peter listened as she explained that Cheryl was brought in about thirty minutes ago and gave him information which he already knew, she had suffered third degree burns to large parts of her body.

'Is she stable?' Peter asked.

The nurse replied in a non committal manner.

'She's stable for now but we won't know how she's doing until she's had time to recuperate.'

'Is there anyone there with her?'

'As far as I am aware her parents have been contacted and are on their way.'

Peter added, 'Are the police watching her?'

The nurse hesitated, 'Yes, there are policemen here.'

Peter felt a sense of relief.

'Okay, thank you.'

He hung up and handed the phone back to Martin.

'Thank you.'

Martin just smiled acceptingly. Peter felt he should explain himself.

'She's not really my sister. I just said that because I knew they wouldn't give me any information if I said I was a friend. We're basically like brother and sister.'

The lie came surprisingly easily. Martin nodded his head as if he understood. Peter shuffled on the spot trying to think of how to ask Martin for a lift to the high street and more importantly why he would tell him he was going there instead of straight to the hospital. He was surprised when Martin, after giving a glance to his wife for approval, offered first.

'Do you want a lift to the hospital?'

Peter smiled thankfully.

'Actually, would you mind taking me to the high street? Her mother lives there, I want to see if she's alright. Apparently, her father and brother are on their way to the hospital now.'

Again, he was amazed at the convoluted storytelling spilling easily from him, but Martin was convinced and nodded.

'Sure, no problem.'

He put his jacket back on and made his way around the car to the driver's side. He looked at his wife, who looked a little concerned, and gave her a reassuring smile.

'I'll be five minutes love.'

'Okay,' she replied simply but her expression said it all, he was to take care of himself with this stranger.

Peter caught the look and offered a smile to the wife as well, humbly bowing his head as he said, 'Thank you.'

She smiled back with her hands crossed over her chest to protect herself from the encroaching cold. Martin reversed the car out of the drive and drove out of the street towards Hyde Avenue. Peter felt the need to thank him again, especially as he felt guilty for luring Martin into this situation under false pretences.

'Thanks again for this.'

'It's no problem. I hope your friend's alright. What happened?' Martin asked and then added, 'If you don't mind me asking?'

'I don't really know.'

Peter tried to stick closely to the truth but not too much as to raise further questions. 'She was attacked by a bunch of kids. She's alright, just shaken up.'

'Jesus, what is it with kids these days? No respect.'

Peter nodded as if in agreement but the sound of police sirens drew his attention. He glanced in the wing mirror and saw a police car coming up behind them. Martin slowed down, turned on his indicator and pulled into the side of the road almost coming to a stop. Peter cowered in his seat a little, tensed as the police car overtook them and sped off up Hyde Avenue. Martin turned off his indicator and moved back into the road.

'There've been a lot of sirens today. I heard quite a few earlier coming from over by the school.'

Peter knew where he meant, the flats near the school, after Colin had died.

Martin continued, 'Is that anything to do with your friend?'

'I don't think so. She was attacked over Low Grange way.'

'Alright, must have been something else. Not much of a lazy Sunday afternoon is it?'

'No, it's definitely not,' Peter replied wistfully.

CHAPTER 24

16:51pm

The rest of the journey was taken in relative silence. As they approached the high street Martin asked where Peter would like dropping off.

'Just at the bus depot would be fine.'

'Are you sure? I can drop you off at the door, it's no problem.'

'No, the depot will be fine. I best get some money in case I need a taxi later.'

Martin didn't argue, 'Okay.'

The bus depot was a cobbled courtyard next to the indoor market just off the entrance to the middle of the high street. Peter knew it was also out of the sight of the police station. He didn't want to go directly into the high street in case there were police roaming the streets.

Martin pulled up by the bus depot and Peter got out of the car. He leant on the door frame and looked in.

'Thank you so much Martin,' he said genuinely.

Martin smiled, 'No problem, I hope your friend's okay.'

Peter smiled back, 'Thanks,' and closed the door.

He stood with his hands in his pockets as Martin reversed and gave him a wave as the car turned and headed away. Peter surveyed his surroundings. The bus depot was quiet, just four buses parked diagonally by the side of the building. In a normal town there would be some signs of limited activity on a Sunday afternoon but in the secluded town of Bilton everything closed down completely. He glanced at the mobile, 4:52pm. The toy store was around the corner and several buildings down the high street, roughly at the half way point between his current position and the police station. Peter could walk down Brunswick Street behind the high street and he would come to a small cut through road called Lodge Street which came out next to Chaser's Toy Store. A brisk wind blew through the courtyard blowing litter and rustling leaves across the shiny pebbles. The orange sun was hanging at the bottom of a dark blue sky, starting its descent behind the horizon. At this time of the year he knew it would be dark in less than half an hour. He started to walk down Brunswick Street remembering the incident in the toy store from their childhood.

Every Saturday the five boys from the Excellent Eight would play five-a-side at the school with their rivals from the year above. The girls would either come along and cheer them on or meet up with them later as they walked into town to browse around the shops. The owner of the store, affectionately known as Old Man Chaser, would promote a different toy each week in the front window. Occasionally it was something good. Peter remembered buying a walkie-talkie set that had worked surprisingly well between Peter's and Cas' houses. They used them to talk to each other at night from their bedrooms even though it was sometimes hard to hear each other as the sets distorted their voices. Peter still had his handset; buried somewhere in a memory box that he kept at home in the attic.

Celo's clue related to an incident that occurred shortly before Bonfire Night. Old Man Chaser had put a display of fireworks in the front window. Even though they were on offer the good fireworks were still too expensive for any of the Excellent Eight to afford. They considered pooling their money but that would only have bought them a few fountain candles and a box of fun snaps. So they decided to do what a lot of children do when they really want something they can't have, steal them. The boys were all wearing T-shirts and shorts as they had come from the game of five-a-side so they had nowhere to hide the fireworks. Cheryl wasn't wearing a jacket either and Laura had a tight fitting denim jacket with no inside pockets. It was decided between them that Michelle should be the carrier of the stolen goods as she was wearing a duffle coat with plenty of hidden compartments for concealing their bounty. She had been reluctant but with some persuasion from Colin, and additional peer pressure, Michelle agreed.

Peter, Cas, Gavin and Laura kept watch, strategically placing themselves throughout the shop like they were on a military assignment. Colin, Steve and Cheryl squeezed and pushed sky rockets and fountains into every available space within Michelle's jacket. With hindsight Peter thought how naïve they were, it couldn't have been more obvious what they were doing. The awkward shapes of the fountains and the sheer amount they had put into her jacket made Michelle look like a tubby hedgehog. As she waddled down the stairs from the first floor towards the exit, four of the group walked in front and the remaining three followed behind her, all eyes darting to and fro nervously as if they were protecting the president. Old Man Chaser watched them come down the stairs, a stern look on his face, and came from behind the counter and approached the group. They picked up their pace, until one of Old Man Chaser's assistants appeared from behind a display in front of them, leaping out like a villain in a horror movie, and blocked their passage to freedom.

The group were all hauled back to the counter by the smug assistant and the angry Old Man Chaser. In front of a gathering crowd of adults shaking their heads and a chorus of disapproving tuts Michelle was forced to publicly empty all the fireworks out of her jacket. Michelle and the other two girls started crying. The boys stood, heads held down, with their lips quivering, fighting back tears. Old Man Chaser was furious, and kept viciously jabbing Michelle in the collar bone with his bony finger as he scolded her and threatened to tell her father what she had done. Michelle flinched and cried louder with every jab and Colin tensed and then flew at Old Man Chaser pushing him away from her.

'Stop it, you bastard.'

He may have been an old man but he was sturdy and he merely shuffled on the spot as Colin pushed him before the assistant grabbed him by the shoulders and threw him back into Peter and Cas who caught him. Old Man Chaser's eyes roved over the whole group, like a warden casting his eye over a line up of convicts.

'Get out of my shop you little shits. And don't ever come back in here or I will call your parents.'

Laura and Cheryl consoled Michelle as the Excellent Eight, not feeling so excellent, trudged through the middle of the parting crowd of adults and jeering children and left the store, never to return.

As Peter approached the cut through he considered what trap lay ahead for him. Colin had been flung out of a top storey window just like the gobstoppers they fired when they were younger. Cheryl was cooked in the oven like the cakes she'd eaten as a child. Peter dreaded to think what consequence stealing fireworks meant for Michelle.

CHAPTER 25

16:56pm

Peter stood in Lodge Street. To his left there was a small pay and display car park, while the toy store building stood to his right. He crept up the small street, sticking to the left side and crossed through the small car park to the corner wall. He cautiously peered around the corner, looking down the high street towards the police station. He couldn't quite see the station as it was tucked behind the buildings on his left, but there appeared to be no activity coming from that general direction.

Peter looked over the street towards Chaser's Toy Store. It was a formidable shop covering three storeys and standing taller than the other two storey buildings in the high street. The faded and blistered red paint of the store name was etched across the side.

It was deathly quiet; apart from the occasional whistling of the wind, which whipped up and down the pedestrianised walkway between the shops either side of the street. All the stores were closed for the afternoon. He left the car park and ran to the side of the toy store and peered around the corner to the front entrance. It was boarded up and derelict, like a number of other buildings on the high street. Above the entrance, and covering the first and second floor - and continuing up to the roof - was scaffolding. Slightly further up the street he saw an empty police car parked next to a butcher's shop.

Peter checked the mobile phone; he had just over thirty minutes to save Michelle. Although he had much longer than he'd had on the other rounds he still felt that he didn't have time to play it safe and wait and see if the officer would return to his car then drive off. Peter took a deep breath and edged round the corner, staying as close to the shadow of the building as possible until he reached the boarded up entrance. He started to investigate the boarding with his fingers to see if he could pull a board open to get in. One of the boards came away easily. He thought that it had obviously been loosened by Celo in preparation for his arrival. He ducked under the boarding and into the disused shop.

The ground floor looked much smaller than he remembered. It used to be a maze of corridors separated by tall shelves packed full of toys. Now it stood empty and deserted, except the floor was covered with crushed cardboard boxes, fragments of glass and pieces of broken toys. The sales counter, where they had been cautioned as children, stood alone at the far end. Even though the room was dimly lit he could see that there was nothing on the ground floor and so he crossed the room, noisily crunching over the glass, and then climbed the curved stairway up to the first floor. The air was dank and foisty and dust particles danced in the thin beams of light which crept through the cracks between the boards on the first floor windows. The light punctuated the darkness and cast shadows over the various counters and empty shelving units. As he took a look around he realised that there were plenty of places for someone to hide. Could Celo be hiding here right now, watching him? He spotted a dismantled shelving unit on the floor to his right and picked up one of the supporting metal bars, clasping it tightly.

Peter tentatively moved down the mouldy carpeted walkway which ran across the entire middle of the floor separating the room into two departments. He had only walked a couple of steps before he froze and his hand instantly tightened on the bar. In front of him was a large supporting pillar. Behind the pillar there was something - someone - casting a person's shadow onto the walkway.

'Michelle?' He whispered.

There was no response. Peter inched towards the pillar, raising the bar by his head like a baseball player ready to strike, his heart thumping faster and faster, almost ringing in his ears.

'Michelle, is that you?' He whispered again, slightly louder.

He paused for a second, took a deep breath and then leapt round the pillar quickly. Standing before him was a mannequin with the painted face of a clown leering at him. He let out his breath in relief and lowered the bar.

A scratching sound echoed out from behind him. Peter reeled around; the bar raised again, his eyes frantically darting to and fro searching for the source of the noise. He shifted up and down the walkway spying between the rows of shelving units which were full of cardboard boxes, blocking his view. The scratching sound came again. He started to move down one of the aisles, holding his breath as he approached the end of the row. He peered around the corner. Nothing there. A rat scurried across a board laid on the floor and disappeared.

He cursed under his breath, 'Damn rats.'

Peter walked around the room's perimeter looking up each aisle in turn. He found nothing. He arrived at the end of the room by the curved stairway leading up to the second floor. Michelle must be on the next floor, he thought.

As if to confirm his thoughts he heard a muffled scream coming from upstairs.

CHAPTER 26

17:02pm

Peter bounded up the stairs two at a time. Three quarters of the way up, as soon as his line of vision passed the top of the stairs, he could see Michelle gagged and bound to a chair at the opposite side of the room. She was partly obscured by a black metal box resting five feet in front of her. Peter scoped the rest of the room as he reached the top of the stairs. There were two windows in the far corner which were completely uncovered throwing a thick bar of pale light across the far wall of the second floor. Through the window he could see the metal bars of the scaffolding. As far as he could see the place was empty apart from the black contraption and Michelle. A mural of a firework display was painted on the wall behind her. As soon as Michelle saw him she began shouting louder beneath the gag and thrashing around as much as her binds would allow.

The black box was similar in design to the one that Colin had been sat on top of, except this one was taller and had a number of circular holes across its face. Peter moved closer and inspected one of the holes; he could just make out the head of a firework mounted in the tube. He turned, to follow its intended trajectory. It was no great surprise to find it was pointed straight at Michelle.

'Jesus Christ.'

Michelle rocked in the chair, fidgeting her arms beneath the ropes which held her there. He rushed over to her.

'It's okay; I'm going to get you out of here.'

He fumbled behind her head, and untied the gag. As soon as it came off she coughed and then shouted in fury.

'What the hell is going on? Is this one of Steve's pranks? It's not fucking funny. I've been here for hours.'

Then she added, 'And I'm pregnant,' as if Peter didn't know.

'It's not a prank Michelle. Someone is playing a sick game with us.'

'What? What's going on? Are you working with Steve? You know.....'

Peter interrupted forcefully, 'Michelle, listen to me.'

He started to pick at the tight rope curled around her left wrist and the arm of the chair. The wedding ring on her finger shone in his eyes. He paused, not sure whether he could tell her the truth as he feared it might upset her even more.

'Listen I'll explain everything but I've got to get you out of these ropes before half five.'

'Why? What happens at half five?'

Peter breathed out reluctantly.

'I think that thing over there is going to shoot fireworks at you.'

'What?' She screamed incredulously. 'Fireworks? What the hell are you on about?'

'It's because you were caught stealing them from this shop when we were kids. Do you remember?'

'Yes, I remember,' she replied instantly as if the thought had already crossed her mind. 'But that was all of us, why me?'

Peter loosened the rope enough for Michelle to free her left arm and he moved over to start on the rope holding her right arm.

'I don't know, I think it's because you were the one carrying them in your coat.'

'You're not making any sense.'

Peter replied slightly irritated.

'Look, someone calling himself Celo is playing this stupid game and everyone has been taken and hidden in places to do with when we were kids.'

Peter instantly knew he hadn't explained the situation very well and his cryptic description would prompt further questioning.

'What do you mean everyone? Who is Celo?'

Peter answered her first question.

'Everyone from the Excellent Eight. You, Cheryl, Laura, Cas, Steve, Colin.'

Peter knew as soon as he said Colin's name what was coming next.

'Colin? Where is he?'

Peter looked up into her eyes as they searched over his face waiting for an answer. His continued silence did nothing to soothe her worries and she started to cry as she asked again pitifully.

'Peter, where is he?'

He couldn't bring himself to utter the words. He couldn't put her through this. An idea formed in his mind, maybe he didn't have to put her through this, at least not yet.

'I don't know where he is Michelle. I can only assume he's been taken like the others …' he lied.

Michelle's tears stopped and she looked at him quizzically. Peter freed her right arm and she took it in turns to rub her wrists. He felt nervous and guilty as another idea formed in his mind. He had already lied to Michelle. She would find out the truth later and hate him for it. So what was stopping him from taking the lie even further and trying to find some answers to the questions he had asked himself earlier?

'Steve is dead,' he said abruptly.

Peter started working on the taut rope around each of her legs and he could feel Michelle's eyes burning into him.

'Steve's dead? How?'

Peter stopped for a moment. He rubbed his brow as he recalled the image of Colin's body plummeting away from his outreached hand towards the ground, the terrified scream echoed through his mind. Peter took another deep breath and continued his lie.

'He fell from the top floor of the flats near the primary school.'

Michelle shook her head. 'I don't understand.'

Peter stared at her, trying to gauge her expression. Did she not understand because she knew it was Colin who died in the flats?

'What do you mean he fell?' She added.

'He was rigged to some device like that box over there which was on some kind of timer and pushed him through the window of one of the flats.'

Michelle held her hands to her mouth and burst into tears. Peter watched as one of her hands instinctively went down and rubbed her pregnant belly. The guilt of his deceitful lie twisted a knot in his own stomach. For a second he debated whether to come clean and tell her the truth. Her grief seemed genuine. He wondered whether the truth would be any better. After all, who did she care about most, her husband or her lover? Michelle sniffed and took a deep breath, wiping her tears away.

'You saw him die? You were there when it happened?'

'Yes. This Celo keeps giving me clues and then he gives me a time limit to find each of you before something bad happens.'

Michelle was silent for a second. Peter continued to watch her as he loosened the rope around her right leg.

'Who else have you got clues for?'

'Steve was first, then Cheryl, now you.'

'Cheryl? Is she okay?'

A few tears welled up in Peter's eyes.

'She's alive.'

Michelle noticed the lack of detail and enquired further.

'But?'

Peter exhaled loudly. He was starting to doubt that she knew anything about this twisted game, and therefore explaining the story seemed to make it more real, as if so far it had just been some kind of nightmare of his own imagining.

'She's badly burnt. She's in hospital now. The sick bastard put her in an oven in a shop over on Low Grange. Remember we used to go there at dinnertimes and she used to buy sweets and cakes?'

'He put her in an *oven*? Jesus Christ, who is this Celo?'

'I don't know much about him. All I know is he's playing a game of Hide and Seek with me. He's hidden all of you and made me the seeker.'

'Why you?'

'I don't know. I've been trying to work that out. What do you remember about last night?'

Peter untied her right leg and moved across to work on the final rope. He stopped for a second to check the time on the mobile phone, 5:11pm. He almost felt a sense of calm coming over him. He had saved Michelle and she was - physically at least - completely unharmed. Michelle interrupted his brief moment of relief.

'I can remember we were at the pub and then we all went back to my house and continued drinking, well you lot did, I was mostly on orange juice … I think I passed out.'

'Apparently we were all drugged, either before or after we got to your house.'

'Drugged? With what?'

'I don't know. It was something that knocked us all out long enough for him to set up the game. Can you remember anything else?'

Michelle thought for a second then shook her head.

'No,' she confirmed.

'And what about here? Can you remember getting here? Did you see anyone?'

'No, I just woke up a few hours ago bound to this chair. Peter I've been so scared. So angry. I thought this might be some stupid prank you guys were playing.'

Peter freed Michelle's left leg and, holding her hands, he delicately helped her up from the chair. They moved away from the front of the black contraption.

'Have you called the police?' she asked as she walked uncertainly, shaking off the numbness in her legs.

'I'm not allowed to involve the police.'

'Why?'

'Celo said that if I involved anyone, especially the police, I would void the game and everyone would die.'

Peter knew what Michelle was going to say next and spoke before she had the chance.

'Not even your father. I don't know if Celo's working with someone from the police.'

'You think my father is involved in all this?'

'No, of course not,' he lied. 'I just don't think all this could be done by just one person. I think he's got an accomplice.'

'Okay, but what on earth makes you think someone from the police is involved?'

'I don't know. It's just a hunch I guess.'

Peter could tell that Michelle was not convinced by his reasoning. He tried to dispel her doubts.

'Look, the police think I'm behind all of this. If they catch me then there's no chance of finding the others alive.'

Michelle was still unconvinced and started to speak but Peter continued.

'I'm on strict time limits Michelle. By the time I explain all this to the police someone else could die. And if Celo is working with someone from the police and finds out I've told them he'll kill everyone else.'

Michelle replied calmly, like a mother speaking slowly to a hysterical child.

'Let me ring my dad. I'll explain everything and make sure he doesn't talk to anyone else.'

'I can't risk it Michelle. I don't know who I can trust.'

'Well you can trust me,' she said as she gave him a reassuring pat on the shoulder.

Peter looked at her, his suspicious mind suddenly replaying his earlier thoughts of her potential involvement. After all, he'd been given plenty of time to save her. He faked a smile. He realised that the smile she was giving him was just as phony. He decided to change the subject.

'First, let's get out of here, and then we'll decide what to do.'

She nodded in approval.

They crossed the room, Peter putting a reassuring arm around Michelle as she limped slightly with stiffness. They moved down the stairs to the first floor.

'Do you have your car keys?' Peter asked as they walked.

Michelle fumbled around in her pockets.

'No … and my purse is gone.'

'That figures, my wallet and phone were taken too. I've had to go everywhere on foot. We need a car to make it easier to get around.'

'Well, my car's at the house and I've got spare keys there.'

Peter remembered searching around the house earlier.

'You're kidding me. Where are they?'

'They're in a drawer inside the wardrobe in the bedroom.'

'Okay, let's go and get your car. I think we have some time before he calls me with his next clue.'

'I still think we should talk to my father. The police have more manpower. They could search the town for the others.'

'That wouldn't work without Celo's clues. The others could be hidden *anywhere*.'

'Peter, it's like you don't even want to involve the police.'

'I told you, Celo said he would kill them all if the police got involved.'

'That's what you say, but how do I even know this Celo character exists?'

They stopped and synchronously took a step away from each other.

'What do you mean? Do you think I'd make this stuff up?'

Michelle didn't have time to answer. They both froze as they heard a crunching footstep on the glass from the floor below them. They darted behind a partition wall. Peter peered out to see a torchlight dancing across the wall of the stairway as someone started to climb the stairs.

CHAPTER 27

17:16pm

Peter was suddenly aware that he had dropped the metal bar whilst helping release Michelle from her bounds. He searched around frantically for another weapon but couldn't see anything of any use. He leaned back against the wall, and looked over at Michelle; her eyes were bulging with real terror.

The figure reached the top of the stairs and stopped. The torchlight beamed past their hiding spot and crept searchingly over the shelving units. Then there was the distinctive crackling of a police radio. Peter assumed that the officer from the police car outside must have returned and seen some movement in the building. Although he felt a sense of relief - that this was the police and not some madman - he remembered he could seek no solace from the police and they had to get out of there undetected. He turned to look at Michelle and found she was stepping back away from him to the furthest side of the partition wall.

Peter looked at her quizzically and mouthed 'Michelle?'

She was shaking her head, visibly upset.

'I'm sorry Peter,' she whispered.

She turned and went around the wall and ran towards the police officer who told her to freeze.

'Help me, I was kidnapped ...'

Peter's heart was racing but he smiled a little. Well done Michelle, he thought. She was buying him time to escape.

'Is the assailant still here?' The deep voice of the officer boomed out.

Peter held his breath.

'Behind that wall,' she whimpered.

Peter gasped in disbelief. He instinctively pushed himself off the wall and darted across the room. The police officer shouted after him.

He bounded back up the stairs to the second floor and came to a stop, frantically looking around for a way to escape. There, through the uncovered windows were the metal bars of the scaffolding outside. He ran over to the spot where Michelle had been tied to the chair and picked up the metal bar again; then over to the window and, covering his eyes with his left arm, he smashed the glass. It shattered outwards onto the wooden boards of the scaffolding. He scraped the bar around the frame of the window to clear the remaining shards. The police officer had not come up the stairs yet and Peter thought he must be attending to Michelle and waiting for backup to arrive. He crouched and stepped through the window frame onto the scaffolding. The bitter cold wind whipped down the tunnel of wooden panels ruffling the green mesh which surrounded the scaffolding. He could hear a commotion coming from further down the street and through the green mesh he saw three police officers sprinting around the corner towards the toy store. As they approached one looked up and pointed directly at him.

'Up there, on the scaffolding.'

Peter took off, his feet clattered and echoed on the wooden boards, as he ran along the front of the building and rounded the corner. There were ladders going up and down. He couldn't go down towards the police so he jumped up onto the ladder, slipping on the rung and banging the side of his face into the metal rungs. He recovered and climbed quickly, head down watching his own feet as he clambered up to the next floor of wooden beams surrounding the roof. From his vantage point he could see across the whole high street and off into the bland suburbs beyond. In the distance he could see the flats standing solemnly. He'd only been inside the toy store for fifteen minutes, but the sky had become noticeably darker. Only the top edge of the sun could be seen on the horizon.

Peter hauled himself onto the roof. He looked down behind him. He could hear the policemen talking to each other but he couldn't see them. He heard a clattering of wood and realised that one of the police officers had got up onto the scaffolding and wouldn't be far behind him. He realised that in minutes the whole building could be surrounded.

Chaser's Toy Store was the last in a row of nine buildings to his left. To his right was a sheer drop down to Lodge Street. He ran to his left and reached the roof edge and stopped short, looking down. The toy store was the only building on this stretch that was three storeys high and he had more than a fifteen foot drop down to the roof of the next building. Peter sat on the edge and manoeuvred himself around to hang down, his face against the wall. He looked down; it was still a decent drop. He let go and landed heavily on his heels, falling backwards onto his behind, scraping the palms of his hands across loose gravel. He rolled over and did a push up to his knees. His heels felt like they had just been hit with a baseball bat. He grimaced as he rose to his feet again and limped over to the next roof edge, hopped over and continued running.

He had crossed another two roofs when he heard a shout behind him. He turned to see a police officer at the roof edge of Chaser's Toy Store. He started talking into the police radio on his chest as another police officer came running up to join him. Peter picked up his speed, sprinting now, and hurdling over the roof edges, until he reached the end building - next to the bus depot where Martin had dropped him off earlier. He looked over the edge and could see the row of four parked buses. He turned and saw that one of the police officers had climbed down the wall and was making his way over the rooftops towards him. The other police officer was still stood on the roof edge of Chaser's, his head cocked into his chest relaying information through his police radio. There was no choice; he had to go for it. He took a few strides back, breathed out and ran towards the edge ...

The drop seemed to happen in slow motion, the top of the bus inching closer. The plastic roof compressed like a bubble and cracked as he landed heavily. He lost momentum and tumbled forward, sliding on his belly across the wet slippery surface. He came to a stop a few inches short of the edge. He was amazed that he was still alive but there was no time to think about what he'd just done. He clambered down the side of the bus and dropped to the ground. He took a moment to relish the fact that he was in one piece, but it was short-lived. A police officer ran past the front of the two buses he was standing between and skidded to a halt upon seeing him. Peter turned and bolted from his hiding place across the cobbled courtyard of the depot as the police officer gave chase.

Peter swerved back onto Brunswick Street running away from Chaser's Toy Store. He sprinted up the street, assessing the roads leading off it and wondering which one to take ... when a blow hit him in the back of the legs. His hands spread out but did little to cushion his fall as the police officer rugby tackled him to the pavement. The sudden impact of his body against the concrete knocked the wind out of him. He had barely time to recover before he could feel the body of the police officer climb onto his back pinning him down. A terrifying panic gripped him as he realised he'd been caught.

CHAPTER 28

17:22pm

Peter writhed furiously as the police officer wrestled with his arms, locking them behind his back. He found a foothold and summoning up the last of his strength he pushed out and bucked upwards like a bull dismounting a rodeo rider. The police man fell forward over the top of his body, smashing Peter's face against the ground. Peter climbed out from under the officer who turned and lunged up to grab the lapels of his jacket. He punched the officer in the stomach but it was ineffective as he couldn't swing properly. The two of them tussled. Peter intuitively grabbed the officer's shoulders and head butted him on the bridge of the nose. He'd never head butted anyone in his life and the collision knocked both of them backwards in equal pain. Peter felt dazed and lights danced in his eyes. He stumbled up to his feet as the officer lay back on the ground holding his nose, thick streams of blood trickling out from the gaps between his fingers. Peter shook his head and started to stumble away from the officer who reached out with one hand and grabbed his right leg. Peter tried to shake off his vice grip. He felt agitated and turned and kicked the officer in the face with his left foot. He immediately felt guilty as the officer cried out in pain. He released his hand from Peter's leg and rolled over cradling his face with both hands. Peter stood over him for a few seconds wondering whether to help him. He was startled as he heard someone shout out behind him.

'You fucking bastard.'

He looked up to the roof he'd jumped from. The police officer who had given chase across the roofs stood watching him. Peter could see him assess the drop, his face a picture of pent up revenge. Peter remembered that there was another police officer somewhere and looked around him but couldn't see anyone. The officer on the roof edge was clearly not considering jumping and started talking into his radio.

Peter started running down Brunswick Street. He took his first right onto Albion Street and took every subsequent turning as he zigzagged away from the scene. Streets and alleyways flashed by and jumbled around him as he ran. He could taste blood in his mouth, and heard sirens whining, but felt thankful that they seemed far away. He had no idea where he was running. There were certain landmarks he remembered as a child which appeared briefly on his run but he didn't register where that placed him in the town. Eventually he could run no more and slowed to a stop in an alleyway behind a row of houses on Auckland Avenue. He collapsed against the outhouse door of one of the terraced houses. He fought to catch his breath as his chest heaved up and down, his entire body racked with pain.

He could hear the sirens of two police cars in the direction of the high street competing against each other, while his attention was drawn to the sky and a patch of clouds seeming to flash erratically as if lightning were going off within them. He could hear the muffled sounds of tiny explosions fizzing like fun snaps going off under a duvet. He pulled the mobile from his pocket - 5:30pm. The firework display rigged to go off in Chaser's Toy Store was firing on time. He had an awful vision of Michelle, still strapped to that chair, the fireworks hitting her with furious force. For a second he wondered if he had indeed saved her, the last twenty minutes had seemed like a blurry dream. He consoled himself that he *had* got to her in time and felt an overwhelming sense of satisfaction. He had saved Cheryl too, but her burns were horrific. So Michelle was his first *real* save, and not only her, but her unborn baby too.

The sense of pride didn't last long - he'd been given so much more time to save her. Could she really be implicated in this nightmare? He replayed as much of the conversation with Michelle as he could recall; tried to reanalyse her reaction. She had seemed very confused when he said he didn't know where Colin was. If she was part of this game she would have known he was the first person involved. Another thing that stood out, in hindsight, was that she had taken a surprising amount of time to ask about Colin. Peter hypothesised that if he had been in a similar situation the first thing he would have done was ask about his wife. Michelle didn't ask about Colin initially, it was only when Peter mentioned his name that she showed interest. Did she delay in asking about Colin because she already knew he was dead?

A doubt crept into his mind. He'd lied about Steve dying, and she'd wept. If she was truly part of the game she would have known that it was a lie. Her tears seemed genuine enough … but could it have been an act? She might have known he was lying, that he was testing her. In a sense her reaction to Steve's death was unsatisfying. She had shed some tears but … it all seemed very *controlled*. And she seemed to get over the news too quickly. She had acted the same with the news about Cheryl. Cheryl was her best friend and yet, when he told Michelle about her being burnt in an oven, she hadn't seemed overwhelmingly surprised or upset. Peter tried to be objective. He couldn't be sure of anything. How could he possibly know for sure how someone was supposed to react to something like this? He wondered at how his perceptions had changed over the last few hours. He felt strangely desensitised from all the horrible violence that had occurred so far.

The most pressing matter: why had she given him up to the police? He'd thought, at first, that she was doing it to buy him time to escape but surely she wouldn't have told the policeman that he was behind the wall if that was her intention. He remembered the look on her face as she pulled away from him, how she'd said she was sorry before running to the police officer. Why had she said she was sorry? Did she not believe his story? Did she think that he was the killer? Or did she just think she would be safer with the police? Even after he had told her that he suspected someone from the police force might be involved? After all her father was The Sheriff. Maybe the two of them were behind this? But for what reason?

Surely he couldn't judge her too harshly. She had just been through a very traumatic experience. But then again, what about him? He had been through terrible traumas as well. He was doing all this alone and had appealed to her for help. She said he could trust her and yet she betrayed him. He had saved her - and her unborn baby - and she deceived him.

He realised that by now she must have been informed that her husband was dead. He recognised that the lies he had told her would probably validate her mistrust of him and justify her actions. He wished he hadn't lied, especially as it had served no useful purpose in the end, and had only confused matters in his mind even more.

He wondered what she was doing now, what she was telling the police. The police would have a fuller picture now. If she'd told them about Celo, perhaps they'd start to help him? At least indirectly, by looking for the remaining members of the Excellent Eight. Peter felt an anxious knot twist in his stomach … but if Michelle *was* involved in this then she could be telling them anything. It would not be difficult to convince them that he was the person responsible for all the atrocities.

Peter rose to his feet and kicked the gravel floor like a petulant child. He hated the possible injustice; he needed a chance to tell the police his side of the story. But it couldn't happen now; Celo had said he couldn't involve them. He had to be selfless; he had to stick to the rules to have any hope of saving the rest of his friends.

Peter stopped for a second and considered this. Maybe he was going about it the wrong way. By playing Celo's game and running away from the police he was making himself the prime suspect. If he had gone to the police as soon as he'd discovered Colin's amputated arm then it would be their responsibility. Why was he putting himself through all this? He had done things today which he'd never thought himself capable of. He had sprinted all over town, on the whims of a madman. He had run across rooftops, jumped from a building onto a bus. He could quite easily have killed himself. He had been involved in a fight for the first time since he was a child and it had been with a police officer. He had done all this to try and save some people he hadn't even seen in over twenty years.

And yet, two of the three members of the Excellent Eight still remaining, meant a great deal to him. Cas was his best friend when he was younger and Laura was his childhood sweetheart. If he was honest with himself, he didn't have much affinity with Steve. He hadn't got on with him too well when they were children due to his incessant sarcastic humour and cruel pranks. In the short time he had reacquainted with him yesterday this only seemed to have gotten worse over time. Steve was still a high priority suspect in Peter's mind, especially as he hadn't come up in the game so far. He wondered why the two he cared about most hadn't come up either. Was that intentional? Did Celo know how much he still cared for Cas and Laura, even after all this time? Did he place them later in the game deliberately? To keep him involved and interested? Of course he did, he thought, all members of the Excellent Eight knew that Cas was his best friend, and everyone knew of his relationship with Laura.

He wondered about Cas, time had obviously changed them both, but he had a wary suspicion about him. He didn't want to believe his own thoughts but he couldn't deny them. Cas could definitely be involved in this but surely Laura wasn't? In all the various conspiracy theories he had entertained throughout the day he had instantly dismissed Laura. He *knew* she couldn't have any involvement in something this horrific. She couldn't

105

be. If he did find out that Laura was involved, that would hurt him the most.

Peter looked up at the sky. The firework display had fizzled out long ago and a thick mist hung below the black sky. He tentatively crept out from the shadows of the alleyway. The street was illuminated with an eerie purple tint and light drizzle began to fall again. Peter's heart sank as he felt a rumble in his pocket, a second before the haunting William Tell ringtone began again.

CHAPTER 29

17:41pm

The distorted voice sounded agitated.

'Peter, you really have to start being more cautious. That's twice the police have nearly caught you. I don't have to remind you what happens if they get involved do I?'

Peter snapped back angrily.

'The police are only after me because of you and your sick twisted games. That's why you chose Colin first isn't it? To involve the police in this from the start? Part of me thinks you want me to get caught.'

'I don't want you to get caught. I've spent a long time setting this up and I want you to have the opportunity to save more people.'

'Bullshit.'

'Peter, I want you to make it to the end of the game. For your own sake as much as mine.'

Peter quizzed, 'What does that mean?'

Celo avoided the question.

'What happened with Michelle?'

Peter wanted to ask him the question again but abandoned it for this new thread.

'You mean you don't know?'

Peter felt a strange sense of relief that Celo didn't know everything this time. He'd felt that Celo had been watching him wherever he went - had seen everything he'd done.

'I saw that she left with the police which was surprising, considering you saved her. Can you remember how much you told her about me?'

Peter instantly felt worried, had he broken Celo's rules by talking to Michelle?

'I had to tell her some things which have happened today,' he stuttered and then added, 'I couldn't tell her that much because I don't know myself.'

Celo was quiet for an uncomfortable few moments before he spoke.

'She might not remember much of what you told her. I imagine she was in a state of shock. And besides there's a very good chance that the police won't believe her anyway.'

Peter bit his lip restraining his anger.

'So what are you going to do?'

'Nothing, for now. We'll just keep moving forward and see if anything comes of it.'

Peter breathed a sigh of relief.

'Anyway, congratulations on saving her. We've reached the half way mark and after being two nil down you've managed to come back and equalise.'

Peter was confused. He asked the question, 'Who's the fourth person?' But he already knew the answer and gasped, 'Gavin. You killed Gavin?'

Celo responded in a matter-of-fact manner, 'Yes, that was me.'

Peter gripped the phone tightly, fighting the urge to throw it away.

'You....fucking bastard,' he shouted.

'I'm sorry Peter but I had to make sure you all came back to Bilton at the same time.'

Peter's fury built up in his throat, choking him.

'I am going to make you pay for this.'

Celo did not rise to the threat.

'Before you embark on a journey of revenge, dig two graves. It seems like you're on my level now. Before today you wouldn't have hurt a fly.'

'I am nothing like you, you sick twisted fuck.'

'We can discuss all this later Peter. But for now, the second half has already started and the clock is ticking again. I know you're angry with me, and yourself, but are you ready to listen to the next clue?'

Peter snarled, 'Go on. Give me your stupid fucking clue.'

Without pausing Celo continued.

'It's a place where you used to go with the boys and the girls. Tired of the football you found it a bore. Bounce on the mats but watch out for the door. Peter Perkins has bad memories of this place. You have till 6:30pm to find and save him.'

This time Peter hung up before Celo could end the call. The words had gone in but all he could think about was Gavin. He thought of all the time he had spent revisiting the old letters and emails to see if there was a clue as to why he committed suicide. It had all been a waste of time - there had been no clue to find. There had been no suicide.

He had felt that something didn't add up, but instead of investigating, he'd just accepted the ruling. He cursed his own laziness. If he had just looked into Gavin's death, like the friend he should have been, maybe he could have prevented today's events somehow. His anger flared. It all pointed back to someone who could cover up the murder and make sure it was ruled as a suicide. He was assured now, more than ever, that someone from the police force must be involved.

He wondered if he could find out which police officer dealt with Gavin's death. He could try and contact Gavin's wife, maybe she would know, but he didn't have a number for her. Maybe he could visit her on the way to save Cas … and only then did his mind's eye focus on the immediate task. Where was Cas? He played the clue over in his head but nothing sprung immediately to mind. He knew it must be something to do with the five-a-side they played every Saturday at the school. He tried to think of a time they had been tired of playing.

'Bounce on the mats but watch out for the door?'

It wasn't jogging any memories.

'Think, Peter, think.'

All the other clues had involved people either hurting themselves or getting into trouble. He tried to think of a time Cas injured himself but could only recall the rugby injury at school when he broke his nose. He and Cas had been in trouble far too many times to recount and his mind went back to the game of Hide and Seek at the Marshalls site. He had been thinking about that earlier and wondering whether it had any relevance to Celo's twisted game and whether it was a clue to his involvement.

Peter wondered if he should start walking towards the school anyway. But if he then worked out the clue and it pointed to another location … he'd run out of time. Again, he wished he had a car. Then it came to him, Michelle's spare keys were in a drawer inside the wardrobe in their bedroom. Should he go back to Colin and Michelle's and take their car? No, he couldn't risk it. Michelle might have warned the police that she had told him about the car.

Peter shuffled on the spot trying to decide what to do next. He *had* to save Cas. He knew if he could, then Cas would help him solve this mess. He wouldn't turn away from him as Michelle had done.

He was still dubious whether the location could be the school. He had passed the school earlier on the way to Low Grange shops to save Cheryl.

This would mean he was doubling back on himself. He had to be careful because the police could still be at the bakery around the corner. His clinching argument to himself was that Gavin's house was near the school. He wouldn't have time to risk going there first but he and Cas could both go there after he had saved him. Peter was surprised at the calmness that had settled on him. He felt sure he was going to save Cas.

He looked at the mobile once more - 5:45pm, Sunday 25th November. For the first time something struck him about that date, as if he'd forgotten something important. Was it someone's birthday? Janine's birthday was 16th January and his son's was 13th April. Was it something to do with why Celo had chosen this day for his twisted game? He racked his brain trying to remember why the date seemed significant but, like Celo's last clue, nothing came to him.

Peter started walking in the direction of the school - almost in autopilot. He added the potential significance of the date to the 'to-do' list growing in his mind and concentrated on the clue for Cas.

'Tired of the football you found it a bore. Bounce on the mats but watch out for the door.'

Then it came to him and Peter picked up his pace towards the school.

CHAPTER 30

17:46pm

The boys of the Excellent Eight had booked a ninety minute session in the sports hall at school to play five-a-side one Saturday afternoon. However, after an hour of getting outplayed by a group of lads from the year above, they finished their game early. The five lads were lying flat out on the ground lamenting their heavy defeat. Steve wandered around the hall and on the off chance he tried the door of the storage cupboard which held all the school's sporting equipment. He was surprised to find it open and beckoned the lads over. As the door swung open and light fell into the large storage area they were greeted with an Aladdin's cave of new toys.

Peter, Cas, Steve, Gavin and Colin found new bursts of energy as they used the twenty minutes they had left to ape around with the equipment. There were four rows of rubber mats, each about eight feet long and wide, which were stacked in staircase fashion. The group took it in turn to climb to the top and perform their most elaborate and theatrical dive down the mats as if they were bouncing down a rocky waterfall. Cas took a running jump and then dived headfirst onto the mats. He bounced off them, turned in the air and clattered sideways into the wooden door of the storage cupboard, sliding down it to hit the floor with a heavy thump. Everyone's immediate reaction was to point and laugh but when he remained slumped on the floor without moving, the laughter died down.

'Cas, are you alright?' Peter said.

He approached the still body with genuine concern.

'Cas?'

Peter put a hand on his shoulder and Cas jerked his body around quickly screaming 'yarrrr!' Peter jumped back startled as the rest of the group burst out laughing.

'Cas, you arsehole.'

He approached again and offered Cas his hand to help him up. They started walking back to the mats and it was only after ten seconds that Gavin noticed something.

'Shit Cas, look at your leg.'

Peter looked down at the same time as Cas to see blood pouring down his left leg from a wound just below his knee. Cas put his arm around Peter's shoulder and started to hop on his good leg. They walked over to a bench and sat down as everyone gathered around them. On closer inspection, they could see the collision had taken a perfect triangular shaped wedge of flesh from his leg.

'Jesus Cas, did you not feel that?' Colin said.

'No, I ...'

'You double hard bastard, that's a right beauty. It's taken a chunk out of your leg,' quipped Steve.

Gavin and Colin went to find the PE teacher, who was supposed to be onsite in case something happened, but instead could usually be found tucked away in his small office, feet up, reading a newspaper.

Mr Carter brought the first aid kit. He was culpable for leaving the door unlocked, so they only got a light scolding for playing in the storage cupboard – then Mr Carter inspected the wound. He cleaned around the wound tentatively before stating the obvious.

'You'll have to go to hospital Cas. It looks like you need stitches.'

The boys were unsympathetic and happily debated amongst themselves how many stitches he would need.

'I'll have to give your parents a call, what's your number?' Mr Carter enquired.

Cas groaned, 'My dad's working, he'll kill me if he has to leave work to take me to hospital.'

'What about your mother?'

'She can't drive,' he lied.

The boys were aware that this was one of the standard responses Cas gave to anyone asking about his mother. They understood that it was simpler than giving a long explanation about her illness. Peter was about to offer to ring his parents, but Gavin offered first and went to the office with Mr Carter to phone them. Fifteen minutes later Gavin's parents arrived and Cas was carried out to the car and taken to hospital.

Peter did as he said he would and called at Cas' house on his way home. He tapped on the door and let himself in, as was customary. The television was blaring out an episode of Last of the Summer Wine and the two bar electric fire was blasting warm air into the room making it extremely stuffy. Mrs Perkins was slumped in a large backed chair, with an air cylinder stood by the side with a tube looping up to a plastic device clipped to her nose. Her chest heaved heavily up and down, her breathing raspy. Upon seeing Peter she fumbled with the remote on the arm of the chair to reduce the volume on the television. She coughed to clear her dry mouth.

'Hello Peter dear.'

She gave her best smile, her discoloured teeth showing between thin lips, and Peter could see it was an effort.

'Hello, Mrs Perkins.'

'Where's my Peter?'

He tried to explain it as best he could, so as to not alarm her, but as soon as he mentioned 'hospital' her eyes widened in shock.

'He's okay Mrs Perkins. He just got a little cut in his leg - it'll need a couple of stitches.'

He refrained from telling her a huge wedge of flesh had been gouged from her son's leg. He sat there awkwardly wondering how to excuse himself. After a lengthy silence he spoke.

'I best get home or my mam will be wondering where I am.'

'Okay dear,' she said with a resigned smile but no argument.

He could tell that she would have liked him to stay longer, if even just to sit and watch the television together without talking. Mrs Perkins spent most of her time in the living room and even slept on the sofa he was currently sat on. Cas' father was often at home, given regular work was hard to come by, but when he was he'd spend most of his time in the backyard tending to his pigeons or down at his allotment.

Peter stopped at the door and turned back.

'Do you need anything getting whilst I'm here?'

Mrs Perkins gave him a grateful smile that said thank you for asking.

'No dear, I'm alright.'

He smiled back. 'Okay, bye Mrs Perkins.'

Peter went home and told his mother what had happened; in perhaps too much detail for his own good. His mother scolded him, lecturing on the 'perils' of messing around. Peter stood, head bowed and nodded at the appropriate times to convince her that he was actually listening.

After devouring a quick sandwich he walked up to the hospital calling for Laura on the way.

When they arrived, Cas, Gavin and his father were in the waiting room. They had to wait there for another two hours before Cas could have his stitches. The children found it easy to make use of the time as they messed about but Gavin's father grew more irritable, looking at his watch every five minutes, and muttering to himself.

In the end Cas had to have ten stitches. When it was over he said the stitches didn't hurt although his eyes were wet and bloodshot. He said the worst thing was the anaesthetic needle they had to put directly into the wound. Cas wasn't the only one who hated needles and Peter, Laura and Gavin all grimaced as he recounted his ordeal.

CHAPTER 31

17:50pm

Peter snapped back to the present and found that he'd walked right through the Auckland Oval estate. He cursed himself at letting his mind wander so much; idly walking around Bilton as if he didn't have a care in the world. He looked around him for signs of life, particularly any police presence, but the streets were quiet. The night had crept in stealthily and it was now dark. Peter walked under a streetlight which highlighted the diagonal streaks of rain. He realised that his breathing was remarkably calm, although his shins were aching from all the walking and running he'd done. He stopped for a moment at the corner of the junction to assess the best way of getting to the school. He decided to cross over and go through Oakfield, an estate comprising a maze of formerly council owned houses in a circle surrounding a large park in the middle. He followed the route in his mind like a ground level satellite navigation plan. He would cut diagonally through the estate to come out by Hyde Avenue, and then cross this main road to enter Low Grange estate again and head around towards the school. Peter crossed over the road and quickened his pace. Through the countless bay windows, people on sofas stretched like meerkats to watch him as he ran past.

Peter wondered why Celo would pick that particular - fairly innocuous - incident over all the other things that Cas had been involved in. Maybe the school was simply chosen out of convenience - closed on a Sunday, it was another empty building in which Celo could rig up another murderous trap. What would it be this time? If it was like the others – and there seemed to be a clear pattern - then how would it relate to Cas slicing a chunk out of his leg? The words echoed in his mind, 'slicing a chunk'. The anxious knot in his stomach - which had surprisingly eased over the last five minutes - tightened once again and he picked up his pace, breathing hard now.

Peter stopped short of coming out onto Hyde Avenue and looked around the corner, up and down the road. It was moderately busy with the gentle hum of cars travelling up to Wolviston or down towards the high street. He could see no sign of police cars. It had been almost three hours since Colin had died at the flats. He had no idea whether the information had filtered through to the local news yet. He imagined news of this nature would spread like wildfire in a small town like Bilton. For all he knew, half the residents might have seen a newsflash about him; the police asking for the public to be vigilant. He thought back to the various eyes glancing up at him from their televisions as he ran through Oakfield estate. He thought back to Martin who had kindly given him a lift to the high street unaware that he was aiding and abetting a wanted fugitive. Maybe he'd now seen the news and was calling the police - his wife telling him loudly in the background that 'you could have been killed.' He looked out at the steady stream of traffic and realised that any one of the drivers or passengers could have heard a bulletin on local radio. Peter felt very alone and paranoid: he the prey, and everyone in the town a hunter. He leant up against the wall of the end terrace, dizzy and light-headed, face tilted to the sky, his eyes closed. He tried to breathe and block out the sounds around him which grew louder, swirling together in a nauseating cacophony. With a deep exhale he steadied himself.

'Keep it together Pete. You're going to cross this road. No one will see you. And you're going to get to the school and save Cas.'

He looked out onto the road again, feeling the ebbs of his panic attack dying down. If there *had* been a newsflash … well, what could he do about it? He had to keep going.

Peter crossed the small grass verge, his feet sinking in the dampened muddy turf, and stood by the edge of the road. He waited for a break in the traffic and raced across.

A sigh of relief died in his throat as a police siren blared out from the road behind him. He froze, panic erupting throughout his body. Would running bring undue attention? He took a few steps forward and chanced a look over his shoulder. The police car flew down the middle of the road, as cars mounted the kerbs on either side to let it through. Peter watched it speed past him, the relief palpable. He walked away from the road and back into Low Grange Avenue.

A quick glance at the mobile phone showed it was 5:56pm. His heart was still beating heavily from the scare he'd just had with the police car. And he'd have to remain cautious - at the end of this road he'd come out onto Low Grange about a hundred yards away from Beamish Road which led to the school - but, just ahead of the turn off, were the Low Grange shops where he had saved Cheryl. It could still be crawling with police.

He couldn't believe that it had only been two hours since he saved Cheryl, the time in-between had seemed like a lifetime.

He reached the end of Chapman Street. He looked up and down the street. Ominously quiet. On his side of Low Grange Avenue there was a row of trees which offered him a little cover and he proceeded to walk down the road as close to the grass verge as he could. He kept his eyes fixed on the hedge on the corner of the turn leading around to the shops as he came closer to Beamish Road. A car door slammed shut behind him and he jumped, instinctively leaning in towards a tree as if he thought it would render him invisible. It didn't, as he turned and looked back up the street he could see a man walking from his car looking directly at him and eyeing him curiously. Peter's heart dropped. The knot in his stomach wound tighter. What if he recognised him? The man gave him a final look with a frown and then began to fiddle with the keys in his hands before opening the front door and entering the house. Peter breathed a sigh of relief. He looked down towards Low Grange shops and upon seeing no activity he crossed over onto Beamish Road and started running towards the school.

CHAPTER 32

18:01pm

The high fence around the school loomed forebodingly. Peter couldn't tell whether it went around the entire perimeter, but he imagined it would. How would he get over it? It had sheer steel posts with curled, spiked tops pointing outwards.

He reached the end of the road and from this vantage point he could see the entire school grounds beyond the fence. It was a relatively small school which looked even tinier sat in the centre of the vast grounds surrounding it. The school itself comprised two L-shaped buildings - three storeys tall and arranged to make a square with entry and exits points at the southeast and northwest corners. Through the darkness Peter could just make out that the fence did indeed surround the entire perimeter. To his right was a lane through the middle of long grass verges which bordered the grounds on one side and provided a small lawn for the back of a row of terraced houses on the other side. He noticed a tree about nine houses down which spruced up right next to the fence. It was his only way in.

There were no low branches for him to grab onto and climb but he noticed that someone had hammered a number of nails into the bark to form a mini staircase. Kids probably used this as their entry point when they wanted to play in the school grounds when it was closed. He felt very exposed again as he looked around. Only a few of the houses behind him had back fences high enough to obscure him. The rest had four foot fences and their rear windows looked directly out onto the school. If anyone walked into any of their back rooms they'd surely spot him. The residents might not be too bothered about seeing kids climbing the tree and jumping into the school grounds but they'd think differently of a man in his 30s. He decided he had no time to worry about that. He had to get going.

The tree leaned away from him so he was able to grab onto it for support whilst he curled his toes like a vulture to get a foothold on the nails. He clambered up the tree quickly to reach the first level of branches which hung over the fence into the grounds. He walked along a thick branch which bowed slightly but was strong enough to hold his weight. He made the small jump over the fence easily but didn't make the most graceful of landings as he hit the ground heavily and rolled forward through the grass. He got up and brushed himself down, no damage done. Of all the running and jumping he'd done today, that was probably the least treacherous of them all. He glanced quickly back towards the houses – nothing there to alert him - so he continued down the sloping hill and trudged across the wet grass.

As he approached the school a security light flicked on, momentarily blinding him. He froze, like an escaped convict caught in a prison spotlight, and then ran forward and pushed himself up against the wall. He waited until the security light went out and inched along the wall, as if on a ledge, and reached the southeast corner. He was agitated to find a padlocked metal gate drawn across the fence. None of this security had been here when he was a kid. He imagined at the northwest corner he'd find the same obstruction. He obviously couldn't climb the walls of the school and the only thing he could think of was a caged off yard round the back where the lads would play football at break times. The children had used to refer to it as the 'bear pit' but he couldn't recall what childhood logic had made them use that term. He imagined it was some reference to wrestling which they were all avid fans of in the '80s.

He ran around the corner and, sticking as closely to the walls as possible to avoid setting off any more security lights. When he got to the rear of the school, he found the gate to the cage was fastened with another padlock. He grabbed it and rattled it angrily. Locked tight. He'd need a key.

A key! He checked his pockets for the keys which Celo had planted for him in Colin's dismembered hand and inspected them. Three keys on the ring and he'd used two of them, one for the flats and one for the shops on Low Grange. Peter tried them all anyway and found that none of them fitted. He stepped back and surveyed the caged yard but the fence was higher than he remembered. It reared up at least ten feet tall. There were bars in a crisscross on the flipside of the gate which would make it easier to climb *out* from the bear pit, but offered no help at getting in.

He wondered if he was missing something. Celo had made it relatively easy for him to gain access to the flats, the shops and Chaser's Toy Store.

He wondered if Celo had done that to ease him gently into his sick game and now they'd passed the half way point it was going to get a lot tougher. He walked around the caged yard trying to find an entry point. The sports hall was the block directly next to the yard where he imagined Cas would be held in one of Celo's garish traps. He looked at his mobile phone again and saw that it was 6:09pm, just over twenty minutes to go.

Peter passed the caged yard and came to the sports hall. Metal guttering climbed up the corner of the wall to the roof. He noticed it was held to the wall with large brackets which would make handy footholds for him to climb up so he could get onto the balcony roof which hung out in front of the sports hall. There was also dark brown paint slapped haphazardly in streaks up and down the guttering and, on closer inspection, he found that it was burglar grease.

'Excellent,' he said sarcastically.

Peter took a deep breath and ran at the wall and jumped up to reach the highest bracket with his hands. He clasped both his hands tightly around the pipe as if he was throttling someone's neck. The burglar grease was slimy in his hands and he didn't feel like he had the strongest grip, but he wedged his feet behind the guttering and climbed up. Halfway up the wall he put one foot onto the balcony roof and swung away from the pipe and clumsily rounded the corner onto the roof. He inspected his hands. They were covered with the tar-like substance from the pipe. He walked over to the wall and rubbed his hands against it. Some of the grease came off but there was a film of mucky brown residue remaining. He tried a few rubs on his trousers and decided that was the best he could do.

From his vantage point he could see that the entire green that used to sit in the middle of the buildings had been paved over. When they were children the green had housed a huge weeping willow which all the kids used to sit under when it was summertime. He felt a slight sadness as he recalled those lazy school days, sitting under the willow tree, cradling Laura in his arms. He looked out past the bear pit to a desolate dry clay field which separated the school from the old mill factory where Cas' father used to work – sitting in darkness, equally desolate.

The field had once been full of six foot high vibrant yellow corn. He recalled playing football and miss hit the ball over the fence and into the corn field. Laura volunteered to go with him and help him retrieve it. Back then it was only a waist high fence separating the school grounds from the field. As they both climbed over it the bell had rung to signal the end of break time. Everyone went inside whilst he and Laura searched the field but ended up kissing each other amongst the swaying corn.

Peter sat down and dangled his legs over the edge of the hanging balcony. He turned and lowered himself down before dropping the short distance to the ground. He was in the courtyard at the front of the sports hall. He walked over to the boys changing room and tried the door and was surprised to find it open.

He crept down the short corridor and through another open door into the changing rooms. Even in the dark he could see that they hadn't changed much. It was a tiled room with lino flooring and benches around all the walls. The showers were behind him and to his left and he glanced around the corner to see if anyone was there. It was empty. He continued through the changing room, down another small corridor which led into the sports hall. As he opened the door he saw a row of light switches and flicked them on to illuminate the empty hall in neon light. He headed towards the storage cupboard, his shoes squeaking on the plastic flooring. The door was slightly ajar and he pushed it open cautiously. The light spilled across the floor and spread up to the far wall which housed a row of four tall lockers and a wooden shelving unit littered with various sporting paraphernalia. The door would only open part way - something behind it was blocking it from going any further.

Peter crept into the storage room and peered behind the door. Another locker had been moved to prevent the door from opening fully, so the far end of the storage room was shrouded in darkness. He searched for a light switch. But found nothing. He went deeper into the darkness, his hands out in front of him, feeling his way forward.

He was about to whisper for Cas when something moved to his left. The shape came lunging towards him. Panic surged through him. In a split second he saw the glint of something metallic bearing down on him and raised his left arm instinctively to protect himself. The bar thudded into his forearm with ferocious force which shuddered through his arm. The impact sent him crashing into the lockers before he slumped to the ground. He looked up as the attacker approached him. Peter felt dizzy, the world starting to blur. He could just see the outline of a man, with the bar raised ready to swing again.

'Cas?' Peter groggily enquired.

The man stopped and lowered the bar.

Peter closed his eyes and drifted off into unconsciousness.

CHAPTER 33

19:19pm

Peter awoke with a start. He was sprawled on the floor of the storage cupboard. The muffled ring of the mobile phone grew louder and more insistent as his hearing ebbed back to normality. The storage cupboard was now fully illuminated; an orange neon light pierced his eyes as he opened them. He winced and tried to sit up. His head was swimming. He felt the same as he did when he woke that morning, as if drugged again. He took deep breaths. The mobile phone stopped ringing. He whispered into the silence.

'Cas?'

He looked around but could see no sign of Cas. He rubbed his face with his hands and felt them lather his face with a warm sticky substance. He withdrew his hands to look at them. As well as the remnants of the burglar grease he saw that his hands were also coated in fresh blood. He glanced down at himself and could see more blood soaking through his shirt. He jumped up to his feet and pulled off his jacket catching one arm in the sleeve then clumsily wrestling it free. He pulled up his shirt to see where the blood was coming from. A quick inspection showed that the blood had not come from him. He massaged his left forearm, where he had been hit by the bar, and sucked air through his teeth in pain as a dull ache filtered through his body. He rolled up the sleeve and inspected the wound. A bright purple rectangular strip was burned across his forearm where the bar had connected. The skin was prickled with burst blood vessels which had risen to the surface of his skin. He clenched his fist and rotated his arm cautiously, testing it. It hurt but he was pretty sure that nothing was broken.

The mobile phone started to ring again. It was not in his pocket, it was perched a few feet away on the wooden shelving unit amongst the sports paraphernalia. He stumbled forward to retrieve it, still feeling slightly groggy. Next to the phone he could see a Bowie knife, like the one used by Rambo, its jagged edged top gleaming with blood. He grabbed the phone and answered it.

'Go to Keithland's Pet Store, hurry Peter.'

Although Celo's voice was distorted, beneath the metallic tones Peter picked up a noticeable concern in his voice.

'Where's Cas? What have you done with him?'

'He's dead Peter. I don't know how he escaped but he was going to kill you. I had to step in.'

Peter's senses sharpened. Celo was different; this had obviously not been part of his plan. He was rattled.

'He wouldn't have killed me.' Peter replied.

'He would have. He clearly thought that you were me. You're lucky I was close by to take over.'

'Where is he?' Peter shouted.

'We don't have time for this. You've been asleep for nearly an hour. It's twenty past seven; you only have ten minutes to save Laura.'

All the questions flying through Peter's mind concerning Cas vanished as soon as he heard her name.

'Where is she?'

Celo repeated what he'd said earlier. He was being direct, no cryptic clue this time.

'She's at Keithland's Pet Store, you have to go *now*.'

Peter pleaded with him.

'I can't get there in ten minutes. You have to give me more time.'

Celo sounded genuinely apologetic.

'I'm sorry Peter. I've been ringing you constantly for the last half an hour trying to wake you. I told you before, I can't amend the schedule.'

Peter shouted back at him, 'This isn't fair. I was knocked out for fuck's sake.'

'Argue with me later Peter, you have to go now.'

'If she dies, I *will* kill you.'

The phone line went dead as he hung up. His gaze left the phone and rested upon the Bowie knife, the silver metal gleaming with reflections from the neon lights above. He grabbed the knife and slid it into his waistband. Putting the phone in his pocket, he ran out of the storage cupboard.

Peter's feet squeaked again across the sports hall floor. Nearly slipping, he burst through the door to the changing rooms which knocked heavily against the wall and almost swung back in his face. He held his arm up to stop it and it clattered against his left forearm sending a shudder of pain through his body. He didn't stop and ploughed through the other door and out into the courtyard. He stopped for a moment to try and work out the best escape route.

The temperature outside had noticeably dropped, more noticeable as he'd left his jacket behind. He remembered the bars on the gate to the bear pit. He sprinted towards it as the bitter wind whistled through his shirt blowing it up like a parachute as he ran. He reached the gate and in one bound jumped up and grabbed onto the top edge of the gate and scrambled up it using the bars as footholds. He swung his body over and dropped down to the ground heavily. Pain sliced through his feet upon impact and shuddered all the way up his legs. The knife in his waistband dug into his thigh. He cried out in pain. He gritted his teeth, picked himself up and carried on - determined - as he sprinted across the field.

'Please, please God. Let me get there in time.'

The security lights picked him up, their beams illuminating the way as he ran towards the perimeter fences. He jumped at the fence but because he'd been running uphill the jump wasn't high enough and he clattered face first into the wall of metal and slipped down it.

'Fuck!' He screamed in frustration.

He composed himself and attempted to climb it again. He jumped from a standing position, grabbing the steel posts, using his feet on the vertical bars to get to the top of the fence. The spike tops which curled outwards were like a mini ledge from this side of the fence. He clambered up onto them and as he did the knife scratched at his thigh again. He took it out and, holding it in one hand, jumped off the fence and landed heavily again.

As he ran down Beamish Road, towards Low Grange Avenue, his hand gripped the knife tighter as anger and hatred filled him.

'I'm going to kill him, I'm going to fucking kill him,' he shouted to himself as he reached the junction of Low Grange Avenue.

He stopped and thought about the distance to the pet store. It was too far away to run there. Now more than ever he needed a car. On the other side of the road a burly man wearing a flat cap was walking a dog. He stood - rooted to the spot now - staring at the knife Peter was brandishing, as the golden Labrador pulled agitatedly on his lead. To his right headlights illuminated the road as a car came around the corner. All the debates and reservations he'd had earlier about stealing a car were now redundant.

He stepped out into the middle of the road, hiding the knife behind his back and held his left hand up in a gesture for the car to stop. The black Fiat Punto screeched to a halt in front of him. He ran around to the driver's side and pulled the door open. The driver was a middle aged woman with stacked permed hair, the curls bouncing around her shocked face. Peter flashed the knife.

'Get out of the car now.'

The terrified woman threw her hands up in a submissive gesture and she started whimpering.

'Get out,' Peter shouted.

The woman fiddled with the seatbelt, her hands shaking.

Peter heard the burly man behind him exclaiming, 'Hey' as he started to approach.

He spun around, pointing the knife at him.

'Stay back.'

The woman managed to release the seat belt. Peter grabbed her arm and yanked her clumsily out of the car, the heels of her shoes clattering against the doorframe, and pushed her away from the vehicle.

'I'm sorry,' he said as he bundled himself into the car and slammed the door shut.

His legs were pressed up against the steering wheel and he fiddled under the seat for the lever to pull the seat back. Outside the car the burly man rushed over to assist the woman, helping her up from the ground as Peter drove away.

The car veered around the corner by Low Grange shops. Peter looked to his right and could see the shops now stood in darkness. The only clue to the horrible incident that occurred there earlier were thin strips of police cordon tape crisscrossed over the door to the bakery shop. He returned his gaze to the road ahead and realised he was going headlong into a police car parked on the corner of the loop in the road. In a panic he veered quickly to his right. The tyres screeched as the car slid sideways across the road. He frantically wrestled with the steering wheel trying to correct the vehicle. The car juddered violently as he crashed into the side of a parked car in a cacophony of noise. And then there was silence.

CHAPTER 34

19:27pm

Peter lifted his head up, dazed and confused. He looked over at the stationary police car on the other side of the road. A police officer came running out of a driveway towards him. Peter snapped back to life and started fiddling frantically with the keys in the ignition as the policeman came towards the vehicle.

'Come on,' he shouted impatiently.

The car shuddered and sparked into life. He crunched the gear stick into gear. The vehicle strained against the resistance and there was the whining sound of metal scraping upon metal as the car lurched away from the accident. He pulled away just as the policeman reached the passenger side, thumping his fist against the window and shouting as Peter drove away.

He looked in his wing mirror and watched as the police officer turned and ran back to his own car. He was in trouble now. The officer would soon be in pursuit and he'd radio the station to tell them he was following the suspect. Or perhaps he wouldn't make the connection. He might just think he was some joy rider. It relieved him slightly, but then he found his anger again.

'They shouldn't even be fucking looking for me anyway. It's not me. I'm trying to save them,' he shouted to himself as he sped down the street towards Hyde Avenue.

As he looked at the speedometer the time display changed to 7:30pm. His heart sank, he hoped that the clock was wrong - ten minutes fast perhaps - that'd be enough, but he knew at best it would only be one or two minutes adrift. As he turned towards Hyde Avenue he could see it was crowded with vehicles travelling in both directions. He had no time to weave in and out of the traffic and so he veered to the left and mounted the curb with a rattling thud. The Fiat Punto bumped along the uneven grass verge which bordered the road, churning up turf and mud. The other drivers did double takes as he drove past them, some of them beeping their horns as if to alert him that he was driving over the grass.

Peter kept glancing at the time display and thumping on the steering wheel begging the vehicle to go faster. He wasn't going to make it, Laura was going to die. What trap might Celo have set up for her? The maniac hadn't given him a clue and had seemed genuinely sorry that he couldn't give him more time to save her. But that did little to help Peter; he had still set up the traps and started this awful game. The importance of Keithland's Pet Store to Laura was obvious, but he couldn't recall any major incident there.

Laura loved visiting the shop and often volunteered to help out so she could spend time admiring the fish in the aquariums that took up an entire wall of the shop. When Peter and Laura were dating he had gone with her sometimes. The owner was Robert Keithland, a spritely man in his mid 60's with a gentle face. He owned and ran the store with his wife, a chatty lady who always spoke excitedly with exaggerated hand movements. The couple knew Laura so well that they let her feed the fish. She'd also help out when they had to transport them to temporary accommodation so the tanks could be cleaned.

Laura was from an affluent family and the other members of the Excellent Eight would sometimes make fun of her for being spoilt. However, for some reason her parents would not let her get her own little aquarium and so she had to make do looking at them in the store. Peter liked them as well; there was something calming about the two of them holding hands whilst sitting on the bench in front of a huge row of tanks watching fish of different sizes and colours flitting about in their protective bubble. He would, however, start to get a little bored after half an hour of counting how many fish were in each tank. He'd always be the first to break the silence and suggest they go into town or back to one of their houses, hoping for an amorous kissing session.

He remembered she would almost be startled when he spoke, as if she was in some kind of trance.

It had come as no surprise to him when she mentioned last night that she'd recently bought her daughter an aquarium. He remembered her smiling coyly when he grinned as she mentioned it, obviously realising that he knew she'd bought the aquarium partly for herself.

He'd thought she might even go on to have a job that involved fish or some kind of sea life. In fact, he recalled asking her once what she wanted to be when she grew up. She had said she wanted to be an ichthyologist. She'd seen the word on the back sleeve of a video for the movie Jaws describing the occupation of Richard Dreyfuss' character. She told him that ichthyology is the branch of zoology devoted to the study of fish, as if she was quoting it directly from the dictionary. He wondered if it was a dream of hers that had never been realised or simply one that had faded away as she grew older. He remembered one time outside her house, standing nose to nose and hands playfully wrestling, he'd asked her if she was studying him what type of fish would he be. She had paused for a second and then said 'a clown fish' before exploding into giggles. He smiled back at her as she laughed, admiring her smile and the way it brightened her entire face and made her blue eyes shine even brighter beneath the blond fringe of hair. The most beautiful smile he had ever seen.

Peter corrected himself. The *second* most beautiful smile he had ever seen. First spot was reserved for his wife Janine. He wondered what she was doing now. He suddenly realised that his train had been due in at 5pm and he should have been back home by half past five. She would be worried about him, but she'd have no idea how worried she should be. No idea of what he was involved in, the things he had done today. Jumping from roofs, stealing cars, being chased by the police and watching old friends die in horrific ways. She'd probably be ringing his mobile phone constantly. But Celo had his mobile. He'd better not have answered it and said anything to her. He'd better not bring her into his sick twisted game.

He could hear a police siren blaring and, glancing in the rear view mirror, he saw the car coming onto Hyde Avenue behind him. The car joined the road instead of driving along the grass verge as he was doing. Now a turn to his right onto Delview Road would take him out of sight of the police car again, if only for a minute or two. Towards the end of that street, just over the railway crossing, was a small row of shops. Keithland's Pet Store was one of those. As he approached the junction for the turn onto Delview Road, he could see cars up ahead slowing down cautiously as they observed a little Fiat Punto churning up mud and turf. Without slowing he reached the end of the grass verge and thumped noisily over the curb and back onto the road. He drove quickly, beeping his horn incessantly, navigating through the traffic like a skier on a slalom course.

'Get out of the fucking way,' he screamed out every time he had to apply the brakes.

The mobile started to ring. He rummaged in his pocket - one hand on the steering wheel - and found it.

'What?'

'If you drive fast enough you can get down the alley behind the shops without the police seeing you. The last key you have will open the front door.'

Peter didn't confirm what he had heard and instead shouted 'Is she still alive?'

'I don't know. There's a chance.'

Celo hung up before Peter could respond.

CHAPTER 35

19:32pm

Peter growled and shoved the mobile into his shirt pocket and returned both hands to the steering wheel as he veered round the roundabout, scraping the bumper of a car meandering around it, and onto Delview Road.

The streetlights illuminated a wide road with little traffic. He pushed his foot down on the pedal, the revs dial leapt up but there wasn't a great deal of acceleration - the speedometer teetering around 70 miles per hour.

Peter wondered why Celo was helping him so much this time. He hadn't offered advice with the others. He had been left to his own devices to resolve any issues he came up against. Even when he had been chased by the police before, Celo hadn't given him any advice on how to try and escape. He wondered if it was because he hadn't been given a proper chance to save Laura. Was it because he was getting close to the end of Celo's game and he wanted him to make it to whatever grand finale he'd devised?

He glanced at the time, 7:33pm. Celo had said there was a chance that she was still alive, his heart fluttered slightly with hope.

The car flew over the railway crossing, juddering over the metal tracks, and an agonising jolt reverberated through the steering wheel and up Peter's tensed arms. He looked in the rear view mirror - no police car - but he could still hear its siren. He was on a decline in the road approaching the row of shops as he braked hard to turn into the alley. The brake pads screamed, and a sickening feeling hit his stomach as the car continued to slide towards the wall of the first building. He frantically turned the steering wheel to the right. The car shuddered as it rattled on the cobblestones of the alley floor and missed the wall by inches and instead veered right towards a fence surrounding the house which lay to the side of the shops. This time he swung the steering wheel left, panicking as he tried to correct the slide. The car came to a violent stop as the side of it collided with the fence accompanied by the sound of crunching wood and splintering panels.

Peter sat there in shock for a few seconds, breathing loudly as he heard the siren getting closer. He tried the keys in the ignition but the engine spluttered and died. He fiddled with the levers by the side of the steering wheel to turn off the headlights. He turned in his seat looking out the back window, hiding his face behind the driver's headrest as if that would conceal him.

The siren grew louder and louder. It was getting closer. Any second now.

Peter could see the reflection of blue lights dancing on the road behind him and breathed in as the police car flew past the alleyway opening. His hands were gripped on the head rest anticipating the screeching sound of brakes as the police man spotted his car. But no screeching noise came. Instead the noise of the siren fell away.

Peter tried to open the driver side door but it wedged against the fence. He clambered over the gear stick to the passenger side and got out of the car. He looked around him; it was remarkably quiet now the carnage had passed. He looked beyond the fence to the house behind it, expecting to see a light come on, but it remained in darkness.

He ran to the front of Keithland's Pet Store. He couldn't believe it was still here after all these years. Even the shop sign, although obviously freshly painted, was exactly the same as he remembered it. He peered through the glass front door. At the back he could see neon blue light spilling out from … something. Something blocked from view behind the rows of cages that housed the rabbits, guinea pigs and hamsters. He noticed that the blue light was rippling across the floor and then realised that the light was reflecting off a pool of water which covered the floor. He remembered that Celo had said the last key would open the door and started fumbling in his trouser pockets. They were empty. A woeful nauseating feeling hit him, the keys were in the inside pocket of the jacket he had left at the sports hall. He started wrestling with the door handle but it was futile. He was just about to put his fist straight through the glass when he remembered the Bowie knife.

He ran back to the car, and searched by the passenger seat where he had dropped it earlier. The knife had fallen underneath the seat and he scraped his hand against the metal under frame as he retrieved it.

He ran back to the shop and holding the Bowie knife, handle outwards, he jabbed at the corner of the window frame nearest the lock. It punched a perfect circular hole clean through the pane of glass and the rest of the window cracked but did not break. He reached his hand through, turned the Yale lock and opened the door. As he entered the thirty second warning of the store alarm started beeping.

'Shit!'

The William Tell tune rang out as if singing along in unison to the alarm. Peter answered the phone and the distorted metallic voice of Celo spoke quickly.

'The code is 4-4-2-5-1.'

Peter flipped the lid of the panel to the right of the door and entered the code whilst speaking aloud.

'4-4.'

Celo repeated, '2-5-1.'

He entered the last three digits and the alarm stopped. Celo hung up without another word.

Peter closed the door behind him and ran in, his feet splashing through the pools of water gathering on the lino floor. Animals rustled in the cages and the screech of a parakeet rang out from the back of the store. He could hear the sloshing sound of water as if a tap had been left running.

Peter rounded the cages to face the source of the neon light.

CHAPTER 36

19:36pm

In front of Peter was a large tank lit up by a neon light within it. Next to the tank was a black metallic contraption, an all too familiar trademark now. The contraption had an arm - like a tap - hanging over the tank and steadily filling it with water. The tank must have been empty to start with but as time elapsed it had filled to the top and was now spilling over the brim.

Peter's face trembled as he started to cry. Grief took hold and he dropped to his knees in the pools of water below him. Lying slumped within the full tank, face pressed against the glass wall, was the dead body of Laura O'Connor. Her hands and legs were bound so she could not punch or kick her way out of her glass tomb. Peter crawled closer towards the tank. Her face was pale white, her mouth open, her lifeless blue eyes staring at nothing. He held his hand up to the glass, which was ice cold to touch, as if he was trying to stroke her face.

Peter mouthed to her, 'I'm so sorry.'

He found it disconcerting that she actually looked at peace. Her face looked serenely calm as opposed to the panic she must have felt as the water grew steadily higher and higher in the tank throughout the day.

He felt the urge to pull her out of her watery grave. He stood up and tried to reach her, but the tank was too tall and he could only grasp at the wisps of her hair. He grabbed a bench, similar to the one they had sat on as children. He scraped it across the floor to the front of the tank, got on top, took a deep breath and immersed the upper half of his body in the tank. He groped under her arms to try and lift her but he couldn't get the leverage he needed from this angle. As he tried, the mobile phone slipped from his shirt breast pocket and sunk to the bottom.

He came out of the tank and started to pound his fists against the glass wall in agitation but it was too thick and did not break. He gripped the top edges of the tank and tried to rock it back and forth. It swayed a little but would not budge enough for him to tip it over. It was stuck fast in a frame which was welded to the floor. He remembered observing earlier how Celo had scored the window in the flats to make it easier to smash when Colin hit it. He fished out the Bowie knife and scratched the blade across the surface of the glass in the shape of an X.

He picked up the bench clumsily, resting most of it under his arm and, using it like a battering ram, drove it into the tank. The glass did not break immediately but cracked and splintered. Peter dropped the bench which thudded noisily off the floor. Trickles of water spat from cracks in the glass like the pierced hull of a sinking ship and then seconds later the entire front of the tank exploded and a torrent of water poured out.

Peter stood firm against the wave of water and caught the body of Laura as the momentum lifted and pushed her body out of the tank. The water spilled down and continued its journey across the floor of the store as Peter collapsed to his knees again, and nestled Laura in his arms. He rocked back and forth, his body tensed and shaking uncontrollably.

'I'm sorry,' he repeatedly murmured between his sobs.

He looked down at her blue eyes, as they stared up at the ceiling. It looked as if she was in some kind of trance, like when she was sat with him staring happily into the fish tanks all those years ago. But he knew this was a trance from which she wouldn't wake. He tried to close her eyelids and was surprised how hard it was. He had seen it done in movies many times before and the person would only have to brush their hand across the person's eyes to close them but it was harder than that in reality. He had to roll her eyelids down with his fingers and it felt like he was closing the shutters of a store. He pulled her body up and buried his head in her sodden clumped hair and wept loudly.

Peter didn't know how long he had been huddled there. It felt like hours as he continued to sway back and forth hugging the dead body of Laura O'Connor. He felt like he had emptied his body of all the tears they could muster and he was now just sniffing and breathing like he was hyperventilating. Behind him the William Tell tune began to play again. He looked around and lying on the floor in front of the tank was the mobile phone, rattling on the floor. He stared at it quizzically; amazed it was still working when it had been dropped in a tank of water. He looked down at

Laura one more time and shuffled her out of his lap and delicately laid her head on the floor. He stretched to retrieve the phone, his face contorting into rage as the anger built up in him.

'You're dead. Whoever you are, I'm going to find you and I will fucking kill you.'

Celo didn't rise to the threat and instead replied with almost genuine sorrow.

'I'm sorry Peter. I know you cared for her deeply. I really wanted you to save her. It might have helped you. But it seems you're destined to lose the ones you care about. If Cas hadn't knocked you out you might have got to her in time...'

Peter interrupted, 'No. Don't you dare blame Cas or anyone else for this. This is your fault. This is all your fault and you're going to pay for it.'

Celo didn't rise to Peter's anger.

'I told you earlier, you will have time to grieve for the people you've lost today. But for now, the game must continue, you're so close to the end now.'

One last person to save, Steve. But a part of him didn't care. He had already lost the people he cared most about. The only person he truly wanted to find now was Celo, so he could kill him.

'You must push your grief aside Peter. I'm proud of you for making it this far. You only have to keep going for a little longer. I promise after this last task you will get your chance to meet me. It's sort of the grand finale to the game.'

Peter did not respond. His face was tense with anger. Steve was still a person, still a human being he could save. And then he would have his chance with Celo, a chance to make him suffer for what he had done to him and the other members of the Excellent Eight. He could have his revenge on Celo for murdering Gavin, for causing Colin to fall to his death, for burning Cheryl, for killing Cas, and for drowning Laura.

'Are you ready for the next clue?'

Peter was momentarily silent. Fixating on his revenge.

'After I do this, after I save Steve, what happens next? You've been setting me up all day. How do I know you're not just going to disappear?'

'At 8:30pm, regardless of whether you save Steve or not, I will call you again with your final clue. Follow the clue and you will find all the answers you've been looking for and I will reveal who I am.'

'How can I trust you?'

'Peter, have I lied to you?'

Peter thought for a moment. Had he?

'I've never lied to you Peter. And I want you to know the truth.'

'Look, I don't care who you are, or what sick twisted reasons you think you have for doing all this. When I find you, I *will* kill you.'

Celo's metallic distorted voice was calm and composed.

'That will be your decision Peter. Someday, you may perhaps come to learn the right and wrong of this. I cannot tell you.'

Peter picked himself up from the floor and with a final sorrowful look at the body of Laura O'Connor he walked towards the exit.

'Get on with it then. Tell me where Steve is.'

'A place where you used to go with the boys and the girls. A graveyard for the ones we abandon, where wars may be lost and won. Steve Jenkins has bad memories of this place. You have until 8:30pm to find and save him.'

Celo hung up. Peter looked down at the phone display - the time read 7:53pm. Celo had left it late to give him the clue. He'd let him lie there and grieve for Laura for over fifteen minutes. An act of compassion or malice? He didn't know. He did know it left him with less than forty minutes to save Steve.

Peter didn't consider the clue that much. He had heard the word graveyard and decided it had to be the cemetery on the grounds of Bilton church. Celo was making him backtrack again; he'd been there earlier in the day when he was chased from the flats after Colin died. He cursed, wishing he'd known then what he knew now. It would have been easy enough to find and save Steve then.

He wondered if there was any significance to finishing the game in the same place where this had all began - with the funeral of Gavin Blair. He was only buried yesterday and yet it seemed like something that had happened weeks, even months ago. Peter remembered that it was Celo that had put Gavin in the ground, feigning his suicide simply so he could get them all back to Bilton to play his perverted game. His anger was almost impossible to contain.

CHAPTER 37

19:54pm

Peter left the shop and closed the door behind him. He glanced down the road - back towards the car he'd dumped. He could see a crowd of people - perhaps five - were gathered at the corner, obviously discussing the accident. He couldn't return to the car, someone would have called the police by now. He had to get out of there quickly.

He turned and started to walk in the opposite direction. He could hear the murmuring of the crowd behind him and the sound of an agitated man cursing. His swearing died down for a few seconds, as did the murmuring of the crowd. Peter had the uneasy sixth sense that they had spotted him. His fears were confirmed when he heard the man shout out.

'Excuse me, you. Excuse me!'

He could hear the man coming towards him - his voice growing louder and more agitated when Peter didn't respond to his shouts.

'Hey, you, stop.'

Peter didn't have time for this and was weary of being chased again. He stopped and turned, pulling the knife from his pocket. The man saw the glint of the blade and immediately stopped.

Peter said simply, 'Fuck off.'

The man - with a wiry frame and designer goatee - held his hands up in submission and started to back away.

'Okay, I'm sorry,' he repeated over and over.

Peter made as if to run towards him and the man turned and ran - back towards the crowd as shocked gasps erupted from them.

Peter himself turned and started running, past the end of the row of shops and round a loop which took him out of sight. He placed the knife back in his pocket as he reached the junction at the end of Delview Road.

He stopped, looking down at himself. His shirt was wet through and covered in blood. His hands were scratched and bloody too, covered in burglar grease. His legs were burning and his shins felt as if someone had hit them with a crowbar.

The cemetery was a good distance away. He didn't know whether he had enough energy in him to run that far. As a car flew past him he wondered if he should steal one again. He felt unsure now. He had done things which he'd never have contemplated ordinarily. He had scared a poor woman from her car at knifepoint and he had just threatened the man outside the shop. In addition, another theft would only alert the police again, and this time they might catch him before he had his chance to find the person responsible for all this and have his revenge.

He started wearily jogging down the road towards Bilton Beck. His legs felt like jelly and every stride felt uneven, as if he was drunk. He stopped after only a hundred yards and bent over gasping for air. The anger and rage he had felt minutes ago had given him a burst of adrenaline but now it had subsided and taken his last ounce of energy with it. There was no way he could run all the way to the cemetery. Then he saw a cyclist coming up the hill towards him. Thoughts raced through his mind. A bike still required effort, would be reported to the police and he'd be out in the open. But there was so little time. He had to act now. He stepped off the curb and put one hand out to stop the cyclist.

'Stop,' he shouted.

The brakes on the mountain bike screeched as the man came to a halt. He lurched forward into a standing position almost going face first over the handlebars. Peter brandished his knife once again.

'Get off the bike.'

The man staggered off the bike and away from Peter. He could see the alarm in the man's face. It was the same flustered terror he had witnessed from the woman he had stolen the car from, the same fear he had just seen in the man outside the shops. The power he felt over them was exhilarating. He now understood what Celo must feel like, having this much control over people's fear and using that to torment them. But he was not Celo and refused to relish in people's misery like he did.

Peter felt guilty and immediately became apologetic. He felt the overwhelming need to explain his actions to the biker, so that he would understand and wouldn't feel the same panicked dread that Peter had felt all day, the same nauseating anxiety which Celo had forced upon him.

'I am really sorry, I need your bike. I'm trying to save someone from being killed.'

The man continued to back away, his hands held up submissively. Peter picked up the mountain bike from the floor and straddled the frame.

'Do you know who I am?'

The man shook his head.

'Have you seen the news today?'

The man shook his head again, his lips quivering as if he was about to start crying.

'The police are after me because they think I've done some terrible things. But I haven't. I'm trying to help my friends. Do you know a man called Steve Jenkins?'

The man shook his head again. Peter had known it was a long shot. Even in a small town like Bilton it was impossible that everyone knew everyone.

'I know it's a lot to ask but please don't report this for at least an hour. If you do and I get caught, a man called Steve Jenkins will die. Do you understand?'

The man nodded enthusiastically in agreement. Peter doubted whether he was actually taking in what he was saying - the man was probably just appeasing him to avoid injury. He repeated himself, just to be sure.

'You can't report this for at least an hour or my friend will die. Do you understand?'

The man continued nodding; adding a few okays as if to confirm that he understood.

'You'll get your bike back from the police later, I promise.'

Peter gave one final glance to the man, looking him up and down and then he looked at his own blood stained shirt.

'Give me your jumper.'

'What?' The man stammered.

'Your jumper, give it to me.'

The man started pulling his jumper off, pulling the T-shirt underneath out of his shorts and getting it stuck on his head as he clumsily wrestled to release himself. If the situation hadn't been so serious, Peter would have found the sight comical. The man pulled off the jumper and threw it to him.

'Thank you.' Peter said.

He threw the jumper on fast but the second his face was covered the man had turned and started running away onto Delview Road towards the shops.

Peter crossed over to the other side of the road and started to ride down the hill towards Bilton Beck. His feet were uneasy on the pedals. He hadn't been on a bike since he was a child. He fiddled with the gears to adjust them down so he could pedal faster and the chains rotated with a clunking noise as he gathered speed down the bank. He turned right at Bilton Beck onto Wolviston Road.

Peter wondered if the biker had truly comprehended what he had said to him and whether he would follow his instructions. He just needed enough time to save Steve and get a head start on his final clue to finding Celo. He thought how much better it would be if the police were actually on his side during all this, instead of him having to run and hide from them. If he'd only been able to tell them from the start what was going on. He felt a twinge of guilt. Had he done the right thing by going along with Celo's game and not involving the police? His record had not been very good. There was nothing he could have done to save Gavin but Colin, Cas and Laura were dead because he hadn't saved them in time. If only he had called the police as soon as he got the first phone call from Celo, or as soon as he had found Colin's dismembered arm. Then the police would have taken it seriously and ploughed all their resources into finding the other members of the Excellent Eight, and maybe more would have been saved. A part of him wished that he could go back in time and make a different decision, but only if he knew that the outcome would have been more favourable. It was hurting him that the whole responsibility for today rested on his shoulders and he yearned for someone else to share the burden with him. If the police had been involved then the outcomes wouldn't have been entirely dependent on him. He shook his head; there was a good chance that the police wouldn't have found any of them, as there would have been no clues from Celo. Maybe he could have involved the police but somehow kept this from Celo. Peter shook his head again. That wouldn't have worked. Celo had been watching him closely throughout the day and would have picked up on any police involvement. Celo had been clear that any involvement from anyone else, especially from the police, would render his game null and void and all the players would die. That was a lie, Peter thought to himself. All the traps had had set time limits. How would he have killed all the players immediately? Peter wondered about Celo's direct involvement in the game. He had obviously set up the traps but on various occasions he genuinely seemed like he wasn't able to change the time limits he had set, almost like he had no control over the game once it was in motion. Perhaps all he could do was sit back and watch? Well, there wasn't much more to watch. He'd find Steve, and then the tables would turn. It would be Celo on the run, and Peter doing the seeking. And when he found the evil bastard, he'd kill him.

CHAPTER 38

20:02pm

Peter had less than thirty minutes to get to the cemetery and save Steve. He wondered what trap would be set up this time. For the first time he went over the words of the clue again, speaking them out loud.

'A graveyard for the ones we abandon, where wars may be lost and won.'

Peter was confused. He could hardly remember ever playing in the cemetery. He could recall playing there once and being chased away by the priest but nothing had happened to them. No one had been caught or hurt.

'A graveyard for the ones we abandon?'

He wondered why Celo would be suggesting we abandon our loved ones when we bury them in a cemetery. And what were the wars that had been lost and won there?

'Shit,' he shouted, screeching to a sudden halt.

In his anger at Celo and in his haste to get going he'd completely ignored the clue and mistakenly thought he had to go to the cemetery. He knew now where he was supposed to go. He had been cycling the wrong way for the last five minutes. He cursed his lack of focus as he turned around and started riding in the other direction. He had to get to Nelson's car yard, on the outskirts of the town, in the desolate industrial estate which lay next to the old mill factory.

In the '80s, when he was a child it was a thriving hub of commerce which supported and manufactured products from the supplies provided from the mill. The Excellent Eight rarely went over to that side of town but occasionally they'd ride out there and use the sprawling network of buildings for games of Hide and Seek as well as retrieving rubble and pieces of wood from the various skips in order to fashion elaborate bike tracks with ramps.

On a few occasions they went into Nelson's car yard. It was a perfect playground for children, with a veritable maze of abandoned cars stacked in rows. They would play made up games within the car yard and the popular movie they would act out was one they made up called Tony and Texas.

In the movie, Tony and Texas were a pair of evil gangsters set on taking over the world and the boys had tracked them down to their lair at the car yard - where they conducted their nefarious deals with other villains. The three girls, Cheryl, Michelle and Laura would play the damsels in distress and pretend they'd been kidnapped and the boys would attempt to save them before they were killed. In reality, the girls used to just sit, talk, laugh and giggle at the sight of the boys as they would pretend fight and battle with multiple henchmen. The boys would make punching noises as they mocked getting beat at first and then they would come back to triumph over the henchmen before facing the evil bosses Tony and Texas.

One day the boys had found that the employees at the car yard had mistakenly left the key in the compactor. They'd played around with the buttons and the conveyor belt had creaked noisily into life. The compactor lay at the end of the belt, its open steel doors looking like the jaws of an upturned mouth waiting to be fed. The boys had no idea how the compactor worked and thought they had only turned the conveyor belt on. They continued to play their made up game. Steve was mimicking fighting a henchman on the conveyor belt. Peter, Cas, Gavin and Colin continued to punch thin air as they fought their respective baddies. They all kept an eye on Steve as he rolled about on the conveyor belt with arms and legs flaying about as he sped down towards the hungry mouth of the compactor. Like a scene in numerous movies they had seen they were expecting Steve would throw the baddie into the compactor at the last minute and it would crush the bad guy in a suitably gory way. The four boys stopped fighting in shock as Steve rolled off the conveyor belt, still battling his invisible assailant, into the compactor.

'Steve, what are you doing?' Colin cried out.

A hand appeared from inside the belly of the beast and Steve started climbing out of the compactor still pretending that he was fighting the baddie. He looked behind him and mimicked the actions of someone kicking a man who was holding onto his leg.

The boys were laughing at his Oscar winning performance when the light in the lantern above the switch to the machine started rotating and flashing and an alarm started beeping loudly. The compactor was triggered by a weight sensor and the jaws started to close. Steve panicked, slipping on the side, stumbling then rolling back inside the compactor. His friends ran to the side shouting for him. Cas jumped up onto the conveyor belt and started running towards the compactor. Colin was the only person who reacted rationally and ran to the switch and thumped the palm of his hand on the red off switch. The jaws of the compactor were almost shut. There was a nervous few seconds as the machine kept going but then it shuddered to a stop. Everybody stood in quiet shock as Cas reached the end of the conveyor belt and looked down inside.

'Steve, are you alright?'

Cas crouched down and lowered his hand to help pull Steve out. Steve looked visibly shaken and Cas held a reassuring arm around his shoulder. Colin broke the nervous tension in the air and spoke first.

'That was awesome.'

The group laughed half-heartedly.

Steve fought back his nerves and quipped, 'That bad guy almost beat me … but I flattened him.'

The group erupted into laughter as Cas and Steve climbed down from the conveyor belt. Although they laughed and joked about what had happened on the way home no one ever suggested going back to the car yard after that, and they never did.

Peter continued down Wolviston Road heading out of town. He knew the road ahead of him would loop right around in a semi circle around the southeast outskirts of the town until it came onto the industrial estate. Ahead of him, to his right, the headlights of a car blinded him. As the car drove past he realised it was a police car without its sirens blaring. Peter's heart dropped and he continued riding, looking straight ahead, expecting the sound of the sirens. But nothing came. After a minute he glanced back over his shoulder - the police car was gone.

He was relieved but also surprised at the ineptitude of the police. They had almost had him in their grasp and chased him on three occasions only for him to successfully escape. He did reason with himself that although this was a small town in which to find him, it was an equally small police force. They were probably more accustomed to babysitting drunken locals and refereeing bickering neighbours than dealing with something of this scale. They would know most of the people in this small town, and yet he had passed right under their noses on more than one occasion today. He was thankful that the police force was not as clinical as the movies he had seen but he reminded himself not to feel too confident. He couldn't push his luck. He still had to be careful. He couldn't afford to get caught now, not when he was so close to the end, and so close to getting his face time with the mastermind behind this terrible game. He didn't need the help of the police now. He didn't need anyone's help. Not that anyone had helped him much today, he thought.

Anger came again as he thought about Michelle's betrayal. He wondered why she hadn't trusted him. Peter could feel himself making excuses for her yet again. Maybe she just had the natural suspicion of a policeman's daughter. Also, at that point, he had been involved in the game for a few hours and had assumed some unnatural calm to override the panic of what was going on. She really had no idea what he'd been through, and furthermore, what he still had to go through after he rescued her from Chaser's Toy Store. Still, he felt she should have had some faith in him; in their friendship. After all he had been risking his own life for that friendship and placing himself in harm's way on multiple occasions. Peter started to wonder about Celo's earlier comment about whether he would prefer to be one of the people who were hiding or to be the seeker. He wondered if any of the other members of the Excellent Eight would actually have gone through all this to try and help the others if Celo had made them the seeker. Some of them had stayed in touch with each other purely by staying in the town but he didn't really know any of them anymore. Was that why Celo picked him? The main person he'd stayed in touch with throughout the years was Gavin but Celo killed him first before the game even started. How did Celo know that he would care enough about the remaining members to go along with his game? The only ones he cared deeply about were Laura and Cas. Peter was sure that Celo placed them towards the end of his game to keep his interest going. Peter started to think about Laura again, but stopped himself. As Celo said, he couldn't get upset now. He would have to grieve for her properly when this was all over.

His thoughts turned to Cas. He had hoped that he could save Cas and then enlist his help. But Cas knocked him unconscious and according to Celo was going to kill him. Surely he wouldn't have done that? Surely he hit Peter because he was scared and confused and couldn't make out who it was in the dark? There was no way Cas would have killed him once he knew it was him. Or could he? Celo seemed convinced that that was what he was going to do. In that case, Peter almost felt glad that Celo intervened and stopped Cas. Peter was still unsure why he did it though. Why was he so hell-bent on having him as the seeker? Peter recalled that Celo had said he was actually proud of him for making it this far. Something twigged in his brain. Cas had made a similar remark to him last night when Peter had told him of his achievements at work. He started to think about it more. After he had awoken from being knocked out by Cas he didn't see his body at any point. He saw no proof that Cas was really dead. If Celo had really intervened why would he have wasted time moving the body? It's not like Celo would have been worried about Peter seeing a dead body bearing in mind the atrocities he had already witnessed that day. If Cas was Celo it would make sense that he would have to place himself in the game somehow to throw him off the scent. Peter recalled that during the few seconds he looked around the storage cupboard when the lights were on; there was no sign of any sort of contraption that looked like a trap which Cas could have escaped from. He had had suspicions about Cas and now everything seemed to be pointing to him. He still couldn't think of a reason why Cas would do something like this, but then again he had searched for answers all day. He hadn't been able to find a viable reason why any of the Excellent Eight would do something like this, specifically picking him as the seeker, and obviously setting him up to take the blame for this game.

Peter felt more determined than ever. He was going to find and save Steve and then he would find and kill Celo, even if it was Cas.

CHAPTER 39

20:12pm

Peter rounded the corner of Wolviston Road on the approach to the industrial estate. To his right, over the uneven hills, hiding in the dark was Durden Woods. The same woods he had awoken in this morning - before this nightmare had begun.

As Peter looked at the closed industrial estate ahead of him he suddenly wondered why he had passed a police car coming from this direction. The brakes of the bike screeched as he came to a stop. He looked behind him but the road was clear and quiet. Earlier he had thought that someone from the police force might be involved and now he had just seen a police car driving away from a derelict site, which also happened to be the same place where Celo had set his next trap. Peter felt uneasy. Maybe he was just being paranoid. Maybe the police car was just doing rounds. But why would someone be doing something as minor as making rounds when surely they must all be looking for the person responsible for today's events? Maybe Celo or one of his helpers was in that car. It would explain why they didn't stop him. Surely, if it was a real policeman they would have been suspicious of a man on his own cycling towards a disused industrial estate at night. Peter became convinced that Celo was in that car and felt angry that he was so close, and had passed right by the person he was seeking. For a second he thought about turning around and going after the car but quickly realised that would be useless, it'd be long gone. There was also the more pressing task of finding and saving Steve.

Peter dismounted and placed the bike against the wall of one of the buildings. The entire site was surrounded by brick walls like a castle, the drawbridge consisting of a metal fence with a chain wrapped around the lock.

He looked beyond the wire fence to the solitary streetlight which lit the road running through the centre of the industrial estate. The fence in front of him would be relatively easy to climb but the barbed wired - looped in circles at the top of the fence - would not be so easy.

Peter took off his jumper and threw it over his shoulder. He started to climb the fence, which was flimsy and bowed inwards under his weight, allowing him to use the horizontal bars on the opposite side of the fence as footholds. He threw the jumper over the barbed wire and delicately used his fingers to pad it down. He winced as he nicked himself numerous times on the barbs. He cautiously pulled himself up onto the jumper and then leapt away from the fence and down onto the street. A sharp pain jolted through his legs as he landed and he yelled out. He shook his legs, trying to shake off the soreness, and jogged down the street past the rows of buildings.

He reached Nelson's car yard. Yet another fence lay in front of him blocking the entrance to the yard. He peered through looking for signs of anything untoward but all he could see was a maze of abandoned cars spread out across the forecourt. Even in the dark he could tell that some of the cars were relatively new models. He deduced that the car yard must still be in use.

'Steve,' he said in a half whisper.

There was no response.

The fence looked harder to climb as it had no footholds and the wire strips of the fence were vertical so he couldn't grip them properly. He decided to climb the wall instead. He took a run up and jumped at the wall, grabbing the top with his hands, and pulled himself up. He heaved his chest onto the top of the wall and lifted his right leg over to straddle it. He realised that the clue which Celo gave him suggested that the trap had something to do with the compactor. He looked out over the car yard again but could still see no clue of where Steve might be. He lifted his other leg over and dropped down off the wall onto the sandy floor of the car yard.

Over to his right was a steel stairway leading up to the office Portakabin. The lair of Tony and Texas, he thought. To his left the forecourt stretched out, seemingly endless with rows upon rows of stacked cars laid out like the shelving units of a supermarket. He walked along looking down each one as if he were searching for the correct aisle to find the last item on his shopping list.

This time he spoke louder, 'Steve.'

He heard the rattling of a chain from the back of the forecourt. A large Doberman came around the corner and, upon seeing Peter, started barking and sprinted towards him.

CHAPTER 40

20:22pm

Peter froze to the spot. As the dog flew down the aisle towards him he could see it was leashed and was trailing a chain which rattled across the ground. He had no idea how long the chain was and whether it would stop the snarling beast before it reached him. He ran to the nearest car and clambered onto the boot and then climbed up the next two cars stacked on top like some giant stairway.

The Doberman reached the first car and stopped. The chain was almost out of length but the dog was close enough. It started jumping, its paws scratching against the passenger side window as it bounced off and came back again.

Peter was stood three cars up on the roof of an old Nissan Micra. The car teetered unsteadily and swayed slightly under his weight. Using the rows of cars before him he cautiously crossed across the roofs making his way towards the back of the forecourt. The Doberman followed below him, barking incessantly. Peter was wary that the noise might attract unwanted attention. He just hoped that because he was in this deserted industrial estate that no one was close enough to hear the commotion and investigate.

After stumbling across the roofs of at least fifteen cars, the dog following him closely all the way, he reached the end of the row. In front of him the car yard still stretched out for at least a hundred yards, full of various cranes and grapples. Towards the back right hand corner he could see the compactor. Even after twenty years he reckoned it was the same compactor and was stood in the same place. Like the dog, its jaws were open.

He looked along the conveyor belt, searching out the switch for the machine. It was covered with a box. The dim light in the yard was still bright enough to reflect off the shiny sleek metallic black surface - instantly recognisable as one of Celo's designs.

The Doberman continued to take run-up's at the car, launching itself upwards. There was nothing Peter could jump onto from his position and there was no way he could get to the compactor without crossing the ground. He looked down from his vantage point at the snarling animal. He couldn't think of any way to pacify it, and he realised, with mounting dread, he would have to kill the dog. He withdrew the Bowie knife from his waistband.

Before he figured out how to get near the dog, the Ford Mondeo he stood on swayed unsteadily as he moved to the edge, and - in a heart stopping moment - Peter could feel the momentum of the car tipping sideways. He crouched as the car lurched outwards away from the car underneath it, toppling like toy bricks.

The Doberman, sensing the impending danger, bolted. And as the car tumbled towards the ground, Peter jumped in midair. He landed on the dusty floor and rolled forward, the knife flying from his grasp. The Mondeo crashed to the ground, and rolled half a turn straight into the bottom car of the opposite row. The resulting smash caused the two cars stacked on top of it to sway and fall away. The second car fell away into the row behind it and the top car dropped down inwards and onto the roof of the Mondeo which was already lying crumpled on the floor. Peter covered his ears at the explosive noise of breaking glass and scratching metal as the cars dropped like dominos around him. It lasted for a few seconds and then there was calm.

Peter rolled over and sat up. A wall of dust rose up from the metal carnage around him. He was about to get to his feet when suddenly the Doberman was upon him. He instinctively raised his arm in defence as the dog sunk its teeth into his left arm at the exact place where Cas had hit him with the iron bar. He fell back and let out a blood curdling scream as the dog's jaws locked on. He used his free hand to try and push the face of the dog away but the jaws remained clamped to his arm. Pain erupted throughout his body, pain he had never felt before. In front of him, laid on the dusty ground was the Bowie knife. He reached out with his other hand to try and grip the handle as the dog shook its head violently to and fro, its sharp teeth tearing at his flesh. He could feel blood pouring down his arm. His fingers teetered on the edge of the knife handle, fumbling to get a grip. The dog let out a gurgling growl as it continued to shake its head. Peter managed to get his hand on the handle of the Bowie knife. He lifted his arm up as high as he could to elevate the dog from the ground. In one swift movement he drove the knife into the underbelly of the Doberman. The dog let out a shrill yelp and he could feel its jaws immediately loosen. He withdrew the blood covered blade and drove it in again; punching upwards with such force it lifted the dog clean off the ground. The dog let out another yelp and released his arm. It stumbled away from him and slumped heavily onto the ground. Peter scrambled away on his backside, clasping his arm in pain. The dog lay on its side, mouth open, fangs oiled in his blood, its tongue lolled out onto the floor. The exposed belly of the dog rose and fell quickly and then slowed and stopped.

Peter inspected his arm. The shirt sleeve was completely ripped open and he could see parts of the flesh on the outside of his arm had been torn away. In the middle were two perfect spherical puncture holes which held pools of dark red blood which shimmered like puddles. He didn't know what to do. He had never been bitten by a dog before. He had seen enough movies to know that he was supposed to wrap something tightly around the wound but he knew what he really needed was to get to hospital. He pulled at his shirt with his good arm, ripping the buttons and tearing his shirt off, wincing as he peeled it off his left arm as delicately as he could. He threw the body of the shirt over his arm and wrapped the two sleeves over and around his arm negotiating them into a knot. He gripped one cuff of a sleeve tightly between his gritted teeth as he pulled the other sleeve with his good hand. The shirt tightened around his arm and he let out a muffled scream. He released the cuff of the sleeve from his mouth and breathed out loudly. He lay there for a few moments waiting for the pain to subside.

He picked up the knife and shakily rose to his feet. He felt woozy and stumbled forward trying to clear his senses. He had only taken a few steps forward when he heard a heavy clunk ahead of him and the sound of scraping rubber as the conveyor belt of the compactor fired into life.

152

CHAPTER 41

20:29pm

Peter stumbled forward to the far end of the conveyor belt. The switch was completely encased within one of Celo's contraptions. He punched at the black box with the handle of the Bowie knife but it would not break. He grabbed the ladder leading up onto the conveyor belt. Every rung he gripped with his left hand sent sharp pains up and down his arm. He screamed through the pain in determination as he climbed the ladder quickly.

He ran down the juddering conveyor belt towards the open mouth of the compactor and stopped at the edge to peer inside. Steve Jenkins was laid curled up on the empty floor, still wearing his suit from yesterday's funeral. A length of rope was wrapped around his wrists and continued down and around his ankles in a figure of eight knot. As soon as Steve saw Peter standing above him, he started squirming on the spot, his eyes bulged and muffled screams rang out from the gag wrapped around his mouth.

Peter was suddenly bathed in light as the lantern above the switch to the machine started rotating and flashing. It was shortly followed by the sound of the warning alarm which started beeping loudly. He jumped down into the belly of the compactor and ran to Steve. Fighting through the pain in his arm again he used the jagged edge of the Bowie knife to saw through the rope between Steve's wrists and ankles. The walls of the compactor hissed and shuddered as the machine started coming to life. He managed to cut through the rope and then went to work on the knot around his ankles. Steve, with his wrists still tied, managed to grab and claw the gag away from his mouth. His first words were succinct.

'What the fuck is going on?'

Dust dropped like rain around them as the compactor doors roared to life and started to close.

Peter cut the rope from around Steve's ankles and pulled him to his feet. He was about to start hacking through the rope on his wrists when he looked up in panic and realised the doors were closing too quickly. The walls of the compactor were closing in.

'Come on,' Peter shouted.

He grabbed Steve by the shoulder and they ran to the exit. Peter jumped half way up the rungs of the ladder leading out of the compactor - stumbling and slipping on each rung as he climbed. Steve followed after him but struggled with both hands tightly tied. The doors of the compactor were more than half way closed and were now folding inwards on their final descent towards closing completely.

Peter rolled out of the compactor as Steve continued to climb behind him. His foot slipped on a rung and he dropped a few rungs back down the ladder. Peter threw out his arms and grabbed Steve's shoulders and tried to pull him up. Steve managed to get half his body onto the conveyor belt which was flowing against him and trying to push him back into the compactor. The doors closed inwards like a Venus fly trap, its teeth inches away from crushing Steve from the waist down. With one last burst of energy Peter leant over Steve's body and grabbed the waistband of his trousers and hauled him out. They both fell back onto the conveyor belt and wriggled away as the doors closed behind them with a resounding thud.

Peter helped Steve to his feet and they ran against the stream of the conveyor belt as they heard the compactor beams crunching together and crushing nothing but air. They climbed down and both of them dropped to their knees in relief as they hit safe ground. As they lay on the floor, taking heavy breaths, Peter asked a question which he realised was stupid as soon as it came from his mouth.

'Are you alright?'

'Of course I'm not alright. What the fuck is going on?' Steve shouted.

'I honestly don't know where to start,' Peter replied.

'Well the last thing I remember was having a few drinks at Colin's house. And then I wake up in that … that thing. I've been in there for hours. I could have fucking died in that thing. Did you lot put me in there?'

'No. We didn't.'

Peter sat up and looked at Steve. He eyed him cautiously. He had suspected him of being Celo, or one of his helpers, at various points during the day but after considering how close he had come to being crushed by the compactor he was unsure whether he could be involved. Steve was looking at the corpse of the dog.

'Did you kill that dog?'

Peter knew that Steve was an animal lover; he was often nicer to them than to humans.

'I had to, it was attacking me. If I hadn't, you'd be dead.'

Steve turned his attention to the blood soaked shirt wrapped around Peter's arm.

'Okay. Still, seems a bit harsh. Couldn't you have just knocked it out or something?'

'Fucking hell Steve. You try and do something nice and humane when you have a Doberman clamped onto your arm.'

Steve had a way of making him feel annoyed as soon as he was in his company, no matter what he said. Peter pulled out the Bowie knife and Steve recoiled from him.

'What are you doing?'

Peter stared at him angrily. The thoughts he had earlier about people mistrusting him weighed on his mind again.

'I was going to cut the ropes off your wrists. Or would you rather stay tied up?'

Steve looked humble and apologetic as he held his arms out. Peter's face softened and he used the jagged edge of the knife to saw through the rope.

'So what *is* going on?' Steve said as Peter finished cutting through the rope between his wrists.

CHAPTER 42

20:34pm

Peter took a deep breath and then tried to explain it as best he could.

'I was the same as you. All I could remember was having a drink at Colin and Michelle's, then I woke up today in some cabin in Durden Woods.'

Steve looked at him puzzled as he started to unravel the remainder of the rope around his wrists.

'Whose cabin was it?'

'I don't know. There was no one there. I thought it was one of your pranks.'

Steve looked slightly hurt at the suggestion. Peter continued.

'Anyway, I walked back to the house and there was no one there. I waited around for a bit because I thought you might have all gone for a pub lunch or something.'

Peter hesitated; he had described the easy bit but wasn't looking forward to explaining the rest. He took a deep breath.

'There was a mobile phone in the house and it started ringing.'

He paused again. Steve was massaging his free wrists and nodded at him to carry on.

'A man, calling himself Celo, said he wanted to play a game of Hide and Seek with me.'

Steve looked at him like this was all a joke. Peter continued.

'Did you feel hazy this morning, like you'd been drugged?'

'Yeah, a bit hazy, I suppose. I thought I was just hung over. I didn't really think about it that much. I was more concerned with being tied up in a fucking compactor to be honest.'

'Well, Celo told me he had drugged all of us last night. He said that he had put everyone in different places all over town and I had to find you all. He's been giving me clues for each of you and a time limit to find you before...' He pointed up towards the compactor. 'Well, before something bad happened.'

Steve stammered, struggling with his words in a mixture of shock and disbelief. Eventually he simply said.

'Why didn't you go to the police?'

'I wasn't allowed to. Celo gave me specific instructions and said that if I involved the police in any way he would kill you all. He wanted me to play the game alone with no help.'

Steve took a moment to consider what Peter had told him and then shook his head, he was clearly unconvinced. Peter decided to interrupt his train of thought and cut straight to the bad news about the others.

'Steve, listen to me. Colin is dead, and so is Laura.'

He held back on telling him about Cas because of his suspicions. Steve stared at him, his eyes moving around Peter's face looking for any sign that he was either lying or joking.

'Celo also said that he killed Gavin just because he wanted us all here so he could play this sick game.'

Steve clambered up to his feet. He looked at Peter repeatedly as if he was going to say or ask something but instead he shuffled around in a circle, exhaling loudly trying to calm down the range of emotions he was feeling. Peter also got up to his feet and waited for him to speak.

'Colin is dead? Wh... How did he die?'

'He was thrown... well catapulted out of the top window of the flats near the primary school.'

Steve stared at him confused.

'Do you remember we used to catapult gobstoppers from the top floor of the flats?'

Steve nodded in acknowledgement.

'Well, they've all been like that. They've all been traps based on things that happened when we were kids. Like you. Remember when you fell into the compactor whilst we were playing in here?'

Peter could tell by Steve's face that he remembered and understood.

'All? Who else has been put in one of these traps?'

'Colin was first and then Cheryl.'

'Cheryl? What happened to her?'

'She's alive but she's in hospital. The sick bastard trapped her in an oven. I managed to get her out but she was burnt quite badly.'

Steve was starting to shake with the enormity of the emotions and he was starting to cry.

'Who was next?' He asked with a lump in his throat.

'Michelle was next, I managed to save her. I think she's with the police now.'

'You *think*?'

'She ran off after I freed her and went to the police.'

'So, she's definitely safe?'

'I think so.'

Steve started to get angry and started shouting.

'You think so? What does that mean?'

Peter started to get angry as well.

'I don't know. I didn't have time to chase after her.'

'What if this Celo goes after her again?'

'He told me he wouldn't, that if I saved them that would be it. I had to move onto the next person.'

'How can you trust this psycho?'

'I can't, but as I said, I had to move onto the next person.'

Steve wasn't happy with Peter's reasoning but after a moment's pause he moved on.

'Who was next?'

Peter took a deep breath.

'Cas.'

'What happened to him?'

'I'm not sure.'

'What do you mean you're not sure?'

'The trap for him was in the storage cupboard of the school. Do you remember when he hurt his leg when we played five-a-side there?'

Steve took a moment to think and then Peter could see him remembering.

'Yes.'

'Well, it seems that he somehow got free of the trap and when I turned up he hit me with a bar or something.'

'Why would he attack you?'

'I don't know. It was dark. I think he thought I was Celo.'

Steve looked at him, encouraging him to continue.

'And?'

'Well, I was knocked unconscious. When I woke up Cas was gone. Celo rang and said that he had to step in and kill him.'

'What?'

'The thing is I never saw Cas' body. I don't know whether he killed him or not.'

'What does that mean?'

'It means I think Cas might be involved in this.'

'Cas? Don't be stupid.'

'The only people it could be is Cheryl, Michelle, Cas or you.'

Steve stared at him, angry at the suggestion that he could be involved. Peter continued with his theory.

'Look, it has to be someone who's still alive. And it has to be one of the Excellent Eight. Cheryl was badly burnt so it's unlikely to be her. And Michelle is seven months pregnant.'

'So basically you're saying it's either me or Cas?'

'No, I don't think you're involved. The compactor came so close to killing you. If you were Celo I don't think you would have put yourself in that much danger.'

'Oh, thanks. Does that mean you suspected me before this happened?'

'I've suspected everyone,' Peter admitted. 'But don't you see Steve? The trap for Cas is the only one which doesn't add up. I didn't even see a trap for him to escape from. And then he knocked me out. Then Celo rang and said he was dead but I couldn't see his body anywhere.'

'But why? Why would Cas do this?'

'I don't know, I've been racking my brains all day and I've still got nothing. But no one has seen or heard from him in twenty years. We don't know what might have happened to him to make him do this.'

'We haven't seen or heard from you in twenty years either, or Laura.'

Peter didn't react to his accusations but Steve stopped as if something had just hit him.

'Did you say Laura was dead too?'

Peter took a deep breath.

'Yes.'

'What happened to her?'

'She drowned. She was after Cas. I was knocked out for too long. Celo wouldn't give me more time and I couldn't get across town quick enough to save her.'

Steve looked at him and scowled.

'Did you really try hard enough?'

Peter's anger built up in a second.

'Fuck you Steve. You have no idea what I've been through. I've been chased by the police all over town because they think I'm to blame for all the shit that's happened today.'

Steve held his hands up in an apologetic gesture but Peter continued with his rant.

'I've been climbing over fences and jumping off fucking buildings. I even threatened some woman with a knife and stole her car to try and get to Laura in time. And I've been bitten by a dog trying to save you.'

'So, I'm the last one?'

The question surprised Peter who had been expecting a retort from Steve.

'What?'

'You've been through everyone else. I was the last one of the Excellent Eight you had to find?'

Peter calmed himself down.

'Yes, you're the last.'

'So it's over now. We can go to the police?'

'Not quite. Well, you can, but I can't go to them yet.'

'Why? You can talk to the police now, there's no one else left to find.'

'There's one left to find.'

'Who?'

'Celo. Whoever he is, I'm going to find him and I'm going to make him pay for what he's done to us all.'

'Are you crazy? Come to the police with me right now. We'll explain everything, tell them about Cas and they'll help us catch this sick bastard, whoever he is.'

'How long do you think it's going to take to explain everything to the police? I can't take the chance that he'll escape.'

'But, even if it is Cas or someone else, how are you going to find him?'

'He said he would ring me shortly after the last game with you. He's going to give me a final clue which will lead me to him.'

'Don't be so stupid Peter. He isn't going to do that. Why would he tell you where he is?'

'He *will* ring. I know it. I think he actually wants me to find him and wants me to know why he's done all this. He sees it as some grand finale.'

'He's had a go at everyone else. So you do realise that if he rings and gives you another clue, it's probably a trap for you?'

'The thought had crossed my mind.'

'And you're just going to walk straight into it?'

'He's worked too hard to frame me for all this to just turn around and kill me.'

'You can't be sure of that.'

'No I can't.'

CHAPTER 43

20:38pm

Steve just stared at him. Peter could see he was working through questions in his mind.

'We should get out of here,' Peter said.

He looked around. He could see the furthest row of cars was stacked against the outside wall. He figured he could climb them - get over the wall that way - and it would save him having to climb both the wall to Nelson's car yard and the barbed wired fence at the entrance to the industrial estate.

'Where are you going?' Steve asked as Peter headed off.

'We should climb over here. It'll be easier than going the other way.'

Steve shuffled on his feet, debating whether to follow him or not.

Peter reached the stacked cars against the wall and wearily started to clamber onto the first bonnet. This last game had taken it out of him more than ever. His exposed body was goose pimpled from the biting wind. His arm was hurting and the burst of adrenaline from saving Steve had subsided and left him exhausted. What he wanted to do more than anything was just lie down and sleep for a fortnight. What he wanted to do was go back home and hold his wife and his baby boy.

He clambered onto the car on the second level. Steve had joined him on the ascent. Peter knew he needed to find the energy for this last part, Celo's grand finale. He knew whatever it was going to be, it could be his biggest test yet.

He reached the roof of the top car and hopped the short distance onto the ledge of the wall and waited for Steve to catch up.

'God, I haven't done anything like this since we were kids,' Steve said as he joined him on the wall.

Peter smiled and nodded in agreement.

'I know, I've been doing all sorts of shit like this today, climbing trees, fences, up guttering. I even escaped from the police earlier by going through Marshalls.'

Steve laughed and then stopped, realising that all this wasn't really a laughing matter, particularly running away from the police. A slight smile remained though.

'Those were good times. Do you remember when Cas got caught by the security guard in Marshalls?'

Peter, without a smile, nodded.

'I was thinking about that earlier, whether it had anything to do with all this. We were playing Hide and Seek in there when Cas was caught.'

'What? You think all this is because he blames us for him getting caught? That seems weak.'

'I know, but I don't know what to think. Whoever Celo is, whether it's Cas or not, he must be doing it for a reason. Maybe it's something we didn't see. Do you know Cas' dad hit him sometimes?'

Steve nodded in acknowledgement.

'Well maybe his dad gave him a severe beating that time,' Peter added.

Steve looked at him, but just shrugged.

'I don't know.'

'Can you think of any other incidents that could point to something? Anything I've forgotten, specifically to do with playing Hide and Seek?'

Steve searched his mind.

'Cas in Marshalls. You broke your leg that time when you fell down the hole in Durden Woods.'

Steve grinned at him.

'You're not harbouring any resentment towards us from that are you?'

Peter laughed, 'No. That was great. It got me out of school for a month.'

If Peter was honest he couldn't remember much about that month but he could recall that he hadn't enjoyed it too much because he missed his friends whilst he was cooped inside the house.

'Anything else?'

Steve shook his head.

'No. Nothing. Actually, we ran away from Laura once. Do you remember, at the mill? Her father rang all our parents to say how nasty we were for leaving her there alone.'

Peter recalled the incident and remembered that she didn't hang around with them for a few weeks after that.

'Oh yeah. I forgot about that.'

'Sorry to ask Peter, but are you completely sure Laura is dead.'

Peter was abrupt in his response.

'Yes. She's dead.'

Steve looked like he was going to ask for more information but decided against the idea and just nodded.

'I'm sorry, I know you two liked each other when we were kids and I could see you both still cared for each other last night.'

Peter was surprised and embarrassed by this comment. He hadn't realised his feelings towards Laura were so obviously visible. Even if they were, the last person he would have expected to notice was Steve 'Joker' Jenkins. He acknowledged Steve's comment with a slight nod and changed the subject.

'Come on. Let's get down from this wall.'

It was a sheer drop of at least twelve feet to the rocky border of the field surrounding the industrial estate.

'Have you got a ladder? Or a parachute?' Steve quipped.

Peter smiled. 'It's not so bad, hang down and we only have to drop about six feet or so.'

'Only?'

They both shuffled around so their stomachs rested on the ledge whilst their feet trailed down the wall. They started lowering themselves down, gripping the ledge with their hands. Peter's left hand was shaking with the pain emanating from the wound on his arm and he let go first and dropped down. He landed on his feet, stumbled and fell over landing on his backside. He let out a tut at himself and thought that after all the times he had had to do that today, he should have really mastered the technique by now. Steve was still hanging down from the wall.

'Are you okay?' He shouted out.

'Yeah,' Peter replied, getting to his feet and dusting his behind. 'Just sick of always falling on my arse.'

Steve laughed and let go, dropping down and landing perfectly on his feet. He turned and smiled at Peter.

'You always were shite at getting down off walls.'

'Cheers Steve,' Peter replied sarcastically.

Steve patted him on the shoulder and they started walking along the outside wall towards the front of the industrial estate.

CHAPTER 44

20:44pm

They were back at the front of the industrial estate. Steve eyed the mountain bike laid on the floor.

'Is that your bike?'

'Sort of. I borrowed it.'

Steve looked at him with his eyebrows raised.

Peter smiled. 'Don't ask.'

Steve nodded in acceptance and picked the bike up.

'So what now?'

'Well I think you should take the bike and ride back into town and go to the police.'

'What are you going to do?'

'I'm going to wait here for Celo's call.'

'You still think he's going to call? You said he would call after you found me and that must have been fifteen minutes ago.'

'He'll call. But I don't think he'll call while you're here.'

'How does he know you're on your own?'

'I don't know. I feel like he's been able to see me all day, like he's watching me all the time.'

They both surveyed the desolate landscape around them and Peter knew what Steve was going to ask.

'Where the hell could he be to see you out here in the middle of nowhere?'

Peter just shook his head and shrugged his shoulders. Steve pleaded with him.

'Don't do this Peter. Come with me back into town and we'll sort this out.'

'No, I'm going to see this through.'

'At least go to the hospital. Look at your arm, it's still bleeding.'

'It'll be alright. I'll get it looked at when this is all over.'

'You're really going to do this?'

Peter nodded.

'You do realise that as soon as I see the police they're probably going to ask me where you are and I'll have to tell them.'

'Yes, do it, chances are I won't be here by the time they get here.' Peter thought for a second. 'Don't stop for a police car. Go direct to the police station.'

'Why?'

'I'm not sure, I may just be paranoid but at certain points today I've been sure that someone on the police force must be helping Celo. As I was coming up to here I saw a police car going the other way.'

Steve looked at him confused.

'So what?'

'Well, what's a police car doing out here at a closed down industrial estate this time of night?'

'Police just drive around all the time.'

'What? During a town-wide manhunt for a killer? And I'm pretty sure whoever was in the car must have seen me but they didn't even stop to check me out, they just drove straight by.'

Steve acknowledged his reasoning.

'Okay, I'll go to the police station.'

He mounted the bike and put one foot on the pedal. He was about to push off when he gave one last uncertain look at Peter.

'Go on Steve, get out of here. I'll be alright.'

Steve pulled off his jacket.

'At the very least take this. It's freezing out here.'

Peter accepted the jacket and put it on. Steve smiled. The small jacket, which fitted his wiry frame perfectly, looked tight on Peter and didn't close properly across the middle revealing his chest.

'You look like a Chippendale.'

Peter smiled.

'Look after yourself and take care Peter,' Steve said with genuine warmth.

Peter responded, 'You too mate.'

Steve nodded and pushed off with the bike and started riding away from the industrial estate. Peter watched the lone figure cycle up Wolviston

Road, disappearing under the blanket of night and reappearing briefly under the glow of the few streetlights dotted along the road until finally he followed the curve of the road out of sight.

Peter stood alone in front of the gates to the industrial estate. Everything was quiet except for the hum of traffic from town and the slight whistling of the wind as it blew across the road rustling the last few leaves and making them dance in the air. Peter could feel the cold and held the jacket closed with his good hand. He looked down at himself and smiled.

'Chippendale. I wish.'

He had been surprised by his rapport with Steve in the brief minutes they had spent together. It was probably the most amiable they had been to each other since they had first met. Peter thought to himself that after the dialogue they had just had, especially under the circumstances, that maybe Steve wasn't such a bad guy after all. However, he did think that once again he was no further forward with who Celo was. He had hoped, at various points in the day, that one of his friends would help him work out who the killer was. Not that it mattered too much now, because the game was over as far as the Excellent Eight were concerned, and now he just had the last task to contend with.

Peter felt a doubt creep into his mind about whether he was doing the right thing. Maybe he should have listened to Steve and just gone to the police. Throughout the entire day he had wanted nothing more than for this game to be over and, in some respects, now it was. Yet he was going on with it, of his own volition. He thought about Steve's remark. Could this grand finale be a trap for him?

Peter's thoughts were interrupted by the muffled sound of the William Tell tune echoing from his pocket.

'This is it,' he said as he pulled out the mobile and answered it.

'Hello Peter.' Celo's metallic voice rang out. 'Congratulations on saving Steve. I knew you could do it.'

Peter responded sarcastically, 'Thanks for putting the dog there.'

'I didn't put Cujo there. He belongs to the owner. He'll be very upset to find his beloved dog dead. I suppose I could have warned you about it though. The bite must really hurt. Believe me, I feel your pain.'

Peter looked around him and wondered how Celo could have seen what happened in the car yard. He tried to remember if he had seen any CCTV cameras in the yard but hadn't noticed at the time.

'Celo, you have no idea of my pain, but you're going to.'

'Still hell-bent on revenge for the ones you couldn't save? Well, you mustn't beat yourself up. You've done very well. I suppose it was unfair for me to add Gavin into the score as I did earlier. After all you weren't really there so we could just say it's a draw at 3-3.'

Peter gripped the phone tightly; his anger level was beginning to rise again.

'Stop pissing around and tell me where you are.'

'Have you ever seen the movie Chinatown?'

Peter was surprised by the question.

'Yes, with Jack Nicholson and Faye Dunaway.'

'That's correct. Jack Nicholson plays a detective called Gittes. He sees something in a pond right at the beginning of the movie. He ignored it and set off looking for conspiracy theories as I'm sure you've had plenty of conspiracy theories on who I am throughout the day. In my opinion, Gittes could have prevented everything that happened if he had only looked more into the gold chain he saw in the pond at the start of the movie. But then again, if he had done that, there wouldn't have been much of a movie would there?'

Peter tried to take in what Celo was saying to him but felt angry at another riddle.

'What are you on about?'

'What didn't you look into when you started the game today?'

Peter remembered where he woke up that morning. As the day had gone on he had forgotten about it completely. He stared out towards Durden Woods as he replied.

'Why did I wake up in the cabin?'

'That's correct Peter. That's where I've been living for the last year. You would have found all the answers there, if you had just looked closely enough.'

'And you're there now?'

'I will be soon.'

'What's to stop me from going to the police right now and telling them?'

'Absolutely nothing. It's your choice Peter. But you do want answers, don't you?'

Celo hung up. Peter stood, looking east towards the woods. A flurry of images raced through his mind. Gavin's funeral, Colin's body hurtling to the ground and landing with a sickening thump, Cheryl's melted flesh as she lay shivering in shock on the floor, Laura's dead eyes staring at him from an overflowing water tank.

He pulled the Bowie knife from his waistband and started running across the field and up the hill towards the woods.

Hiding in the darkness at the corner of Wolviston Road, a person leaning against the fence observed him as he crossed the field.

CHAPTER 45

20:44pm

Peter reached the edge of the woods and climbed over the ramshackle fence that bordered it. He looked up at the trees which towered above him. He moved silently through the woods, listening for any sound. He could barely see anything, and wished he had a torch. He hadn't paid that much attention to where the cabin was and he wondered if he could find it again. He knew he had to find the main trail through the woods and find it from there. Peter crossed over the last piece of unsheltered land and entered the woods.

His feet crunched over the dead leaves that littered the floor of the forest. He looked around him cautiously as he walked, surrounded by layers of thin barks, barren of leaves, standing like giant matchsticks. He stumbled repeatedly on the uneven ground.

This is it, he was thinking to himself. After all the events of today, he had reached the end of the trail and still had no idea what to expect. He considered each member of the Excellent Eight, searching his mind for any last clues which could prepare him for what might come next. Gavin had died first, before he arrived in Bilton. His mind flitted through movies he had seen with unusual plot twists and wondered if anyone had actually seen his body. Could Gavin be alive? There was no chance that it could be Colin, the image of him falling to his death from the top floor of the flats played out in his mind again. Cheryl couldn't possibly be involved. If she was, then she'd made an almighty sacrifice in allowing herself to become badly burnt. He wasn't sure about Michelle. By now she would have discovered that her husband was dead, and if she didn't trust him before, she certainly wouldn't trust him now because he had lied to her. But was she involved in this anyway? It was hard to imagine a heavily pregnant woman being involved in such a heinous crime, but after all the events that had occurred today he decided that nothing could be ruled out and nothing would surprise him. Cas was next, his main suspect, but he had no idea why he would set up an awful game like this. Something must have happened to him during all those years where they'd lost touch, but why hold a grudge against the Excellent Eight? The possibility that maybe Cas was just a psycho; that there might not be a wholly logical reason for all this did cross Peter's mind.

And then there was Laura. Peter felt an overwhelming sadness and guilt come over him again. If Cas was responsible for all this, not only had he put Laura in harm's way in the first place but he had also knocked him unconscious and therefore prevented him from having a decent chance to save her.

Finally, there was Steve. Peter didn't know what to think about Steve. He had come very close to being crushed by the compactor. Peter suddenly considered something he hadn't thought about earlier. Maybe there was a failsafe on the compactor. He shook his head; he had heard the compactor crushing thin air after they had both escaped from the jaws of the mechanical beast. Still he wondered if maybe he should have confronted Steve a little more, maybe tried to trip him up somehow like he had tried earlier with Michelle. In the movies, if a killer was pretending to be someone else they would usually slip up by saying something which they couldn't possibly know, therefore revealing themselves to be the killer. Peter read back over the conversation like it was a transcript in his mind but nothing unusual stood out. If Steve was involved, Peter had just let him walk away from the situation.

Peter climbed a small steep embankment and emerged onto the main walking trail which cut through the middle of the woods. The ground was cold and hard like clay and he kicked up dust as he started walking down the trail, further into the heart of the woods.

Peter had considered all of the Excellent Eight: Cas was his main suspect, and Steve was number two on his list. And what if it wasn't someone from the Excellent Eight? Whoever Celo was, he knew a lot about the escapades they got up to as kids but that didn't mean for certain that he was a member of the Excellent Eight. Again, he thought of something he should have asked Steve. Had he or any of the others spoken to anyone about their exploits? Maybe Celo had quizzed Gavin before he faked his suicide. It seemed a little unrealistic but it wasn't beyond the realms of possibility. Was someone from the police force or the medical profession involved? He had considered it on more than one occasion today. It could be both. He had only spoken to Celo - which suggested that only one person was behind this madness - but he had no real idea how many people could be involved. The overriding question remained though, why?

Peter continued down the winding trail in the darkness. Ahead of him he could just make out the stump of a tree resembling a headless body sat down with its two arms hanging in midair. He remembered seeing the same tree shortly after he had left the cabin that morning. This was the point where he had joined the trail after leaving the cabin.

Peter left the path, heading back onto the uneven ground of the woods. His feet continued to crunch on the fallen leaves carpeting the forest floor. Diagonally ahead of him, coming from deeper into the woods, he could hear a slight rumbling noise like the sound of a petrol lawnmower. He continued walking and as he passed by a clump of trees he could see a light ahead which he surmised was a window of the cabin. He tried to recall whether any lights had been turned on when he was there that morning and decided there weren't. If a light was on, somebody must be home. His hand clasped the handle of the Bowie knife as he walked forward towards the cabin. The rumbling sound grew louder as he approached.

Peter stopped twenty yards short of the cabin, under cover of the trees and surveyed the landscape around him. He realised that the rumbling sound he could hear was the sound of an electric generator coming from behind the cabin. He considered his options. Should he just walk in through the front door? What if it was a trap, as Steve had said?

He hunched over and scuttled forward towards the cabin and rested against the outside wall. He crept towards the window and peered in cautiously. The light was coming from a tall lamp standing next to the couch. There was nobody in the living room. He continued to watch, searching for any sign of life. Nothing happened. He looked to the other side of the front door, for any sign of a trap, but he couldn't see anything that looked unusual or out of place.

Peter moved to the door of the cabin and, standing against the frame to protect himself, he turned the handle and pushed it open. He hid as the door creaked and swung into the living room of the cabin. Nothing happened.

'Coming, ready or not,' he whispered.

He took a deep breath and walked inside, tensing and bracing himself for an attack. Nothing happened. He crossed over the living room and as he passed by the lamp he glanced down and noticed that the plug of the lamp was attached to a timer switch in the socket.

'Shit,' he said under his breath.

There might not be anyone here after all.

He looked into the bedroom where he had woken up only hours before. The bed was still unmade and flakes of mud were scattered across the floor from his muddied shoes. It didn't look like anyone had been here since him. He continued into the small bathroom. The dirt rimmed bath sat there, the tap dripping slowly the same as it had that morning. The cabin was empty. Although Peter's immediate feeling was a sense of relief that no one was here this was quickly replaced by frustration.

'Where are you, you bastard?'

He stood in the middle of the living room. He pulled out the mobile phone and checked the time; the display read 9:03pm. Celo hadn't given him a time limit for this particular part of his game and now he regretted not asking him. He wondered if it was in keeping with the other clues he had had that day which was normally an hour. If that was true he was early for the first time today, and by his reckoning he would probably have to wait until 9:30pm.

Peter sat down on the couch and the plastic material of the cushions squeaked under his weight. The day had been so hectic and frenetic that he found it strangely uncomfortable to find himself waiting for something to happen.

He looked around the cabin. It was extremely bare. No television, no pictures on the wall, a few shelves hung from the walls but nothing on them. Whoever lived here certainly didn't bother themselves with trinkets and basically lived off the bare essentials.

In the silence and lack of activity Peter could feel the dull throbbing pain in his arm grow. He lifted up the sleeve of the jacket and looked at the shirt tied messily around his arm. Two patches of red had bled through the entire material of the shirt to the surface. He stood up and walked to the far corner of the cabin, which constituted the kitchen, and checked in the cupboards hoping to find a first aid kit. The cupboards held only the minimum of crockery, a couple of plates and mugs. There was no food. There seemed little hope of success, yet - in the last cupboard he checked - Peter found a green metal box containing first aid items. He took off his jacket and gently unravelled the shirt from around his arm. He ran the tap for a few seconds and then clenched his fist to tense his arm as he held it under the flowing water. He delicately stroked away the dry blood from around the two wounds as the water mixed with his blood and sloshed down the plughole. Now the majority of blood was gone the two puncture wounds looked even deeper and nastier than earlier. He turned off the tap and using the clean parts of the shirt, dabbed carefully around the wound to dry his arm. He took two large plasters out of the tin box and shuffled them uneasily over the wounds. He then took a bandage from the box and wrapped the whole roll around his arm. With a last grit of his teeth he tied the ends of the bandage tightly around his arm. He exhaled as the pain subsided. He inspected his handiwork.

'Not bad.'

He turned the tap back on and cupped handfuls and splashed his face, before taking a few much needed mouthfuls of cold water.

Peter put the jacket back on and was about to cross the room to the couch when he saw the black metal ring laid flat across the door to the basement of the cabin.

He remembered what Celo had said about the movie Chinatown. He had said that Gittes could have prevented everything that happened if he had only looked more into the gold chain he saw in the pond at the start of the movie. He had opened the door that morning but hadn't gone down into the basement. An anxious knot twisted in Peter's stomach. He picked up the Bowie knife from the kitchen worktop and moved to the door. Going down on one knee he gripped the handle and threw it open.

CHAPTER 46

21:08pm

The basement door clattered noisily as it thudded off the cabin floor. Peter stared down into the black hole. The cat litter box smell wafted up to his nose again and he scrunched his face in disgust as it stung his nostrils. He retched slightly.

He moved over to the tall standing lamp by the couch, removed the shade and carried the lamp back to the basement door. The wire of the plug wasn't long and didn't reach so he laid it on the floor with the bulb as close to the door as he could get it.

He could now see the top few steps of a wooden staircase. Peter stepped onto the top stair and ducking down he started to descend the staircase. In the slightly illuminated path he could see a wall at the bottom, with the rest of the basement behind the staircase. He tentatively continued down the stairs, wary that at any moment a hand could come between the exposed stairs and grab his legs.

He reached the bottom and turned to peer into the dark basement. His sixth sense told him he was alone, but he didn't feel certain. Something was dangling in front of him, something metal which glinted slightly in the low light emanating from the lamp at the top of the stairs. He reached out and grabbed it. It was a light switch cord. He yanked the chain and a single light bulb came on, illuminating the basement.

He had been right; there was no one down here. The room stretched out ahead of him taking up half the space of the living room above him. The floor was covered in an old carpet, which looked oddly familiar. It was faded red and adorned with patterned swirls of black that looked like mini crop circles. At the far end sat a large desk, like an artist's desk, which was covered in various folders and pieces of paper. Above the desk he could see a map of Bilton pinned to the faux wood effect laminate wall panels. To the left of the desk was a workbench and adorning the shelves around it were numerous work tools such as drills, hammers and saws. To the right of the desk stood an empty cage, which rose from the floor to the ceiling. It looked like a bird cage you would find in a pet store. The floor of the cage was uncovered and the ground was disturbed, as if it had been dug up recently. Amongst the churned earth he could see white crystal chunks that sparkled in the light. There was no mistaking that the smell was coming from those crystals. He imagined being inside that cage … trapped, cowering in the corner, shivering and crying.

He walked towards the desk. He could now make out marker pen circles and colour coordinated pins highlighting specific areas of the map on the wall. His heart dropped as he recognised the places: the flats, Low Grange shops, a building on the high street, the secondary school, a building on Bilton Green, the industrial estate. A giant X marked a spot in Durden Woods which he surmised was the location of the cabin itself.

'Jesus Christ.'

If he'd only come down here earlier he would have discovered where the Excellent Eight had been hidden. Peter could feel tears welling up inside him. He could have saved all of them.

He flicked through the paperwork on the desk. He could see sketches and blueprints for devices. His heart dropped again as he recognised one of them, the contraption shaped like a catapult which had thrown Colin from the top floor of the flats. A stack of files lay at one end; the top file had Gavin Blair written across the front. He lifted it up to look at the one below - it had Colin Clark written on it. He continued rifling down and seeing all the names of the Excellent Eight - in the exact order that they had taken part in the game.

He opened Gavin Blair's file. It contained scraps of paper covered with notes about Gavin. He skim read and realised they were descriptions on his personal life, that he was married with children, recollections of incidents that involved Gavin as a child and notes on medication that could be used to cause cardiac arrest.

He picked up Colin Clark's file. It was essentially the same, but included smaller, rudimentary sketches of the catapult contraption. Peter saw that amongst the text on the page, the story of Colin falling down the stairs at the flats was circled, and the clue which Celo had given him was scrawled next to it.

Peter dropped the file, he felt sick. He leant over the desk, breathing heavily, his world was revolving again. Peter took a few moments to compose himself with deep breaths.

He opened the desk drawers and looked inside. They were full of medical journals and textbooks. Could it be possible that he'd taught himself the things he had needed for his sick game?

Peter moved over to the other side of the desk and rifled through the drawers there. He found a certificate of course completion entitled Emergency Medical Training.

The name of the recipient on the award was Peter Stevenson.

He was confused. Why was his name on this certificate? He turned it over, feeling the quality of the paper and rubbing his thumb over the seal on the front to try and ascertain whether it was a fake. He concluded that if it was counterfeit it felt like a very high quality forged document. He continued looking through the drawer and found an ID badge for Bilton General Hospital. The name on the badge was Peter Stevenson.

He started to back away from the desk, as the world started spinning again.

'He's stolen my identity.'

He had suspected that Celo was framing him; this – sickeningly - confirmed it. And then it struck him … was Celo going to turn up here at all?

Thoughts were racing through his head. Is that why Celo had put him here in the morning and led him back here? His fingerprints would be all over the cabin now. He had just touched all the files on the desk. The police would assume he – rather than Celo - had been using this as his den, to devise his sick game. Celo *wasn't* going to turn up after all. He had lied to him. He should have gone straight to the police; he should have gone with Steve.

Peter hadn't noticed the sound of footsteps creeping down the stairs behind him. But he did hear the click of a gun being cocked, ready to shoot. He froze, terrified. His eyes darted frantically around the basement, it was no use, there was nowhere to hide. Celo had turned up after all and was going to kill him.

CHAPTER 47

21:17pm

Peter raised his hands in a submissive gesture and closed his eyes expecting the worst. He thought of his wife and his son and felt regret that he would never see their bright smiling faces again. He heard the sound of more footsteps on the floor above him. Celo was not alone.

'Don't you fucking move,' the man on the stairs shouted out.

Peter opened his eyes. The man behind him wasn't Celo. Peter felt the cold steel of handcuffs wrap around his right wrist.

The police officer pushed him forward roughly and shoved his face down on the desk. He pulled his arm down behind his back and then grabbed Peter's left arm. Peter winced as a bolt of pain from the wound jolted up his arm. The police officer handcuffed his hands together.

'We've got him,' he shouted up the stairs.

Peter could hear a cacophony of noise and commotion as numerous police officers came down the stairs whilst others ran about upstairs checking the rooms. The police officer grabbed his wrists hard and yanked him up straight.

'Come on you bastard.'

Peter didn't say a word as he was led up the staircase back to the ground floor of the cabin. His mind was racing.

Armed police officers stood in a row, watching as he was led through them like a celebrity on the red carpet walking between gathering fans and journalists. Only the faces weren't looking at him adoringly. The feelings of malice were evident on all their faces, so much so that Peter thought they might start spitting at him. He felt angry and the injustice built up inside him.

'It's not me. You've been chasing the wrong man you fucking idiots.'

One of the officers, a large man whose gut poked out from the bottom of the bullet proof vest he was wearing, lunged at him.

'You sick bastard.'

A commotion of noise broke out as his colleagues grabbed him, wrestling him away from Peter as his fingers clawed at his neck trying to strangle him.

'For fuck's sake Adams, control yourself,' a senior officer shouted at him.

Peter was led away as the colleagues of Officer Adams gave him reassuring pats on the shoulder and calmed him down as he continued to stare steely-eyed at Peter.

As he was escorted from the cabin there were more police officers stationed outside. He had never seen so many policemen and women in his life. The officers who had stormed the cabin were obviously some form of armed response unit - no doubt drafted in from the nearest city to apprehend him. As he was led away Peter thought about the evidence they would collect from the cabin; evidence which pointed squarely at him.

'You have the wrong man,' he shouted as he was bundled into the back of a police car.

CHAPTER 48
Monday 26th November
03:01am

Peter paced impatiently around his cell. The initial interrogation had been surprisingly brief. He had waived his right to have a solicitor present - eager to tell his side of the story so that the police knew the killer was still at large.

He'd tried to recount the entire day's events to The Sheriff and was aware that his ramblings seemed unlikely and incoherent at best. He was aware that he'd jumped from event to event in no discernable order and went off on tangents as the incidents presented themselves in his mind. The Sheriff had managed to restrain his emotions and remain professional the majority of the time. However, every now and then, Peter had noticed him scowl especially when he talked about the death of Colin and the threat to his daughter. After he was placed back in the cell he had initially sat down and tried to work back through the day so he could explain it better to the officers when the questioning inevitably continued. However, what composure he had gathered, was now lost after a long, nerve-wracking wait. Now he just felt angry at himself. He knew he'd been set up and given all that happened during the day he was irritated that he couldn't pinpoint *one* piece of evidence which could prove it was Celo and help them find the real killer.

For the last half an hour Peter had stopped thinking about the day's events and he was thinking about Janine and George. In his haste to recap the day's events he had forgotten to ask for his one phone call. He wondered if they had been contacted yet and if so, whether they were on their way to Bilton. How much information would The Sheriff have revealed to her over the phone? He felt regret that his wife had to hear the news from the police. He imagined how scared and upset she must be and wondered what was going through her mind as she drove to Bilton to be with him in his hour of need.

The police station had been a commotion of activity over the last few hours. Peter wondered if they'd acted on his information and whether they were any closer to finding Celo. He heard multiple footsteps echoing up the corridor growing louder as they approached his cell. The iron bolt creaked back and the door slid open. The Sheriff appeared with an officer he had seen earlier, and an older man sporting a white beard and glasses. He didn't look like police.

'Come with us Peter,' The Sheriff said and escorted him back towards the interview room.

'Have you contacted my wife?' Peter asked The Sheriff.

The Sheriff didn't respond, simply looked towards the older man. Peter was perturbed by The Sheriff's reaction. His mood was noticeably uncertain, but he managed a sympathetic smile to Peter.

'No. Not yet.'

Peter was led into the interview room and took his seat. The Sheriff pressed the record button on the tape recorder.

'Interview commenced ten past three am on Monday 26th November. For the benefit of the tape, present are Chief Superintendent Heron, Superintendent Creedy, Doctor McNulty and Peter Stevenson.'

A doctor? They must think he was crazy.

The Sheriff withdrew from the table and stepped back to the corner of the room with his colleague, arms folded. Peter's eyes moved from The Sheriff to the doctor sat at the table. He had a yellow foolscap folder in front of him and fiddled with the edges as he spoke.

'Hello Peter, I'm Doctor McNulty.'

Peter just nodded agreeably.

'I'd like to talk to you about the incident that occurred in Durden Woods when you were thirteen years old.'

Peter stared at him, puzzled.

'What incident?'

'The incident when you fell down a hole in Durden Woods.'

He took a few seconds to remember what the doctor was referring to.

'What has that got to do with anything?'

'It's important Peter. I'd like you to recall for me what happened to you in August 1992.'

Peter was confused by the doctor's request but decided to go along with it.

'We were all playing Hide and Seek in Durden Woods. I was the seeker and the others ran off to hide. I was looking for them and fell into some kind of dug out hole, like a bear trap or something. There were branches covering it and I didn't realise and fell through. I broke my leg on the way down so I couldn't climb out.'

'How long were you in the hole for?'

'I can't remember, a few hours I think. It got dark so … it must have been hours.'

'Where were the others? Didn't they come back and find you?'

'No, they ran off and left me in the woods.'

Peter had a sudden realisation that they still believed he was the killer and that the doctor might be trying to establish some obscure motive. The very idea seemed preposterous.

'What? You think that I'm angry with them for leaving me in the woods as a kid? You think that has something to do with what's happened today? That's ridiculous. It was just a prank. We'd done the same thing to Steve a few weeks before in the flats.'

'Done what?'

'You know, he was the seeker, we said we were all going to hide but we just ran off and left him there.'

'Okay, but weren't you scared to be left alone in the woods?'

'I can't remember. I suppose so. I was in pain from the leg.'

'What happened next?'

'A man found me. I suppose he heard me shouting and he helped me out of the hole and took me home.'

Doctor McNulty paused for a moment, looking down at the folder laid out in front of him.

'Do you remember who the man was? Or what he looked like?'

Peter thought for a moment, he had never really considered the man before. All he could picture was a big strong man, wearing a cap. He recalled that the man had a beard but couldn't picture his face. Peter remembered the man towering over him, the feeling of coldness seeping from the walls around him, enclosing him. He shook his head as he realised his memories couldn't be right. The man hadn't come down into the hole; instead he had lifted him out by hand. He struggled to think again, this time he could see that the walls weren't made of mud either. They were made of faux wood effect laminate wall panels. He felt confused, he was jumbling up images. The doctor interrupted his thought process.

'Peter? What do you remember about the man?'

'I don't know, I can't remember who he was. That's awful isn't it? Considering he helped me out of the hole and saved me.'

Peter smiled slightly and looked at the doctor and then The Sheriff and his colleague, no one smiled back.

'What happened next?' the doctor asked.

'Nothing, the man carried me back home. I went to the hospital and, as I said, I had a broken leg. And that's all that happened really. I was in the hospital for a few days and then I had to have a plaster cast on for six or seven weeks.'

The doctor opened the foolscap file and pulled out a newspaper cutting and handed it to Peter.

'I would like you to take a look at this and tell me what you think.'

He looked at the newspaper. It was the front page of the *Bilton Courant* dated 18th August 1992. The main photograph was a grainy picture of a large bearded man wearing a cap being led away by police, one either side of him. Peter started to read the article.

After a 15-day, town-wide search, the man arrested in connection with the kidnapping of a thirteen-year-old boy was revealed to have been a 'dangerous individual' who should not have been allowed on the streets. Robert Paulson, a 49-year-old father of one, was still being questioned by detectives last night.

The boy was found in the basement of Paulson's cabin in Durden Woods where he was locked in a cage. A passer-by walking his dog raised the alarm after hearing pleas for help on Sunday morning.

The incident has left residents of the area shaken ...

Peter looked back up at the doctor quizzically. The doctor stared at him with his eyebrows raised, as if expecting him to have some kind of revelation. Peter started to feel a dark sense of foreboding as images of the man who had rescued him in the woods flashed through his mind again. He didn't want to ask the question because it made no sense to him, but he felt like he already knew the answer.

'Who was the boy?'

Doctor McNulty's face softened in sympathy.

'Peter, the boy was you.'

CHAPTER 49

03:18am

Peter leaned back in his chair, staring at the doctor for some sign that this was some kind of sick joke. The doctor continued.

'Have you heard of dissociative identity disorder?'

Peter stammered, 'What, like schizophrenia?'

'The two have similarities but are not quite the same. Let me explain. Someone who suffers a severe sexual, physical, or psychological trauma can disassociate themselves from the trauma by fracturing into two personalities. This is especially common if the person experiencing the trauma is a child. You see Peter, when we are children we are still developing a personality structure. So a severe trauma can greatly interfere with a child's natural character development and can condition the brain to form dissociative identities. It's quite common for there to be one host personality, but an alternate part of the personality can become dominant and take control of an individual's behaviour. When this occurs it is also common for there to be an associated memory loss, which is why you have no recollection of these events.'

Peter shook his head incredulously.

'This is complete bullshit.'

He waved his arms around gesturing to the officers.

'Do you really believe this shit he's coming out with?'

The Sheriff and the officer both stood stone-faced. He returned his attention to the doctor.

'Let me get this right. You're saying this boy in the paper, this boy who was abducted was me and I can't remember it because I created an alternative personality?'

'Yes, and in comparison to other cases I have seen it was an effective defence mechanism. More than half of the people diagnosed with dissociative identity disorder go on to have various physical and physiological problems. Yet you did not. And it appears that your alternate personality did not manifest itself again until about a year ago. I believe you call him Celo.'

Peter sat back in his chair looking around the room as it swirled around him. Everything felt simultaneously close and yet far away. He now realised that if the story about him as a child was true, they were using it to implicate him in the day's events. Celo must have known that this would happen; he must have really done his homework.

'He's got you all fooled. Celo is not an alternative personality. He's real. I know he is. I've been speaking to him on the phone all day.'

'Peter, you just imagined you were speaking to Celo but you were really speaking to yourself.'

Peter looked at him bemused and shook his head.

'People do it every day, they talk to themselves,' the doctor added.

'This is bullshit. Plus you said if an alternative personality takes over then the other forgets everything. Now you're saying I'm having delusions and speaking to my own alternative personality?'

The doctor was about to speak but The Sheriff broke his silence and barked impatiently.

'Look. You can't have been talking to anyone on the phone because it didn't even have a SIM card in it.'

Peter stared at The Sheriff as a frantic feeling of paranoia swept over him.

'What? That can't be right.'

He pointed accusingly at The Sheriff.

'One of your men must have taken it out. One of your men is involved in all of this.'

The Sheriff responded in a matter-of-fact manner.

'I was the one who examined your phone, and there was no SIM card in it.'

'Liar,' Peter shouted rising from the chair.

'Sit down,' The Sheriff shouted.

The doctor interjected, 'Please calm down Peter.'

'Calm down? This is a fucking conspiracy. Can't you see that? Why am I asking you? You're probably in on it as well.'

'Sit down,' The Sheriff repeated with more authority.

Peter observed The Sheriff's twitching fingers hovering near his baton. He took his seat again and the doctor continued.

'There is no conspiracy Peter. Your alternative personality set up and arranged this game of Hide and Seek.'

'No. Cas has something to do with this. I'm sure of it. Have you found him yet?'

The doctor took a second to compose himself before speaking.

'Peter, the police found his body in the women's changing room at the school. He's dead.'

Peter stared at him in shock.

'It wasn't me. I was unconscious.'

'I believe that Cas' escape was clearly not part of Celo's plan and so when he attacked you Celo became the dominant personality and killed him.'

Peter tried to recall what happened. In hindsight it did seem strange to him that being hit in the arm and falling against the lockers would be enough to knock him unconscious. Plus it hadn't happened immediately, he remembered feeling groggy like he had felt when he woke up in the cabin.

'I killed Cas?'

'No Peter. Celo killed him. He was the one who planned and started this whole game.'

'But I don't understand how he could have set all this up? I've only been here since yesterday.'

'Actually, it's likely that you've been in Bilton for more than just one day Peter,' the doctor replied.

'What?'

'When the police found out who you were they checked on the PNC and found that you were reported missing almost a year ago.'

'What's a PNC?'

'The Police National Computer.'

'And it says I've been missing for a year? It must be wrong.'

'It's not wrong Peter. You've been missing for a year and we have good reason to believe that you have been living at the cabin in Durden Woods for at least the past six months.'

'Why?'

'Because Robert Paulson was released from prison in May.'

Peter sat upright. 'What?'

'The cabin in Durden Woods belonged to Robert Paulson. The police have found a body buried under the cage in the corner of the basement. It was covered in quicklime to mask the smell.'

Peter recalled the smell coming from the white crystal chunks amongst the disturbed ground on the floor of the cage. The doctor continued.

'It's too early to tell, but we believe forensics will show it to be the body of Robert Paulson. We think Celo came back here and killed him as retribution for what he did to you. And then buried him in the cage where he held you captive as a child.'

'Look, I'm not going to lie. If it is this … Robert Paulson, then I'm glad the bastard is dead, but I can't have been here for the last six months. I can prove where I was last week. Ring my company. I've been working late nights with a team of people for the last month to get a contract bid finished. Ring my wife Janine, she'll tell you. We all went to Blackpool Zoo last Saturday.'

'I'm not saying these things didn't happen, but they didn't occur in the last year. It is common for the host personality to take memories out of sequence or fabricate new memories to explain and validate the period of time where the alternate personality is in control.'

'But wait a minute. You said I'd been missing for a year but then you said Robert Paulson was released in May and that I've only been in Bilton for six months. What was I doing for the other six months? Are you saying I was Celo before Robert Paulson was even released from prison?'

'Yes.'

'But why? After more than twenty years why would I suddenly change personalities completely out of the blue?'

'People relapse for a number of reasons. The most common is when the host personality suffers another traumatic event which it cannot cope with. In this scenario the host personality disassociates itself from the event and the alternate part of the personality becomes dominant as a coping mechanism.'

'Another traumatic event?'

Doctor McNulty paused to take a deep breath.

'Peter, does yesterday's date, 25th November, have any resonance with you whatsoever?'

He thought back to earlier, when he was entering Low Grange and heading towards the school. Something had seemed familiar about the date, like he should be remembering something that happened. He searched his mind again but it was blank.

'Yes, there's something familiar about the date. I've been trying to remember all day, but I don't know.'

Out of the corner of his eye Peter could see The Sheriff and the other police officer shifting uncomfortably on the spot, as if they knew what was coming. He looked at the doctor who was already trying to give him a reassuring and comforting smile. A lump formed in his throat as he realised there was obviously going to be another revelation to upset him.

'What is it?'

The doctor retrieved a piece of paper from his folder and slid it delicately across the table.

'I'm sorry Peter, but your wife and son died on 25th November last year.'

Tears came as he looked at a copy of his wife's death certificate. The doctor placed his hand on Peter's trying to comfort him.

'How?' he sobbed.

'Brake failure. They were involved in a head-on collision with another car.'

CHAPTER 50

04:00am

The Sheriff and the other officer escorted Peter back to the cell. He collapsed onto the bed, shuddering as the waves of emotions rippled repeatedly through his body. Through the grill on the door The Sheriff watched as he curled up on the bed, hugging the quilt which spilled out above his arms and covered his face.

The Sheriff closed the grill and walked back into the interview room where the doctor was reading another document contained in his folder. The doctor, aware that The Sheriff was staring at him in silence, looked up.

'Yes?'

'So basically he's insane?'

'He's had a mental breakdown.'

'How is all this going to affect his conviction?'

'His lawyer is likely to plead diminished responsibility and with all the evidence of his condition on file, coupled with the loss of his wife and son, the court will probably accept the defence.'

The Sheriff scowled. 'That man killed my son-in-law and almost killed my daughter. And you're telling me he'll probably just get thrown into Broadmoor?'

The doctor nodded in acknowledgement. 'I'm sorry.'

'I can understand why he'd come back here and kill Robert Paulson after what he did to him but why this game of Hide and Seek with my daughter and her friends?'

'I won't know for sure until I can speak to his alternative personality but I have a theory. I listened to the recording of the interview from earlier. Peter said that Celo kept telling him this game was an opportunity to save the people he cared about. I believe Celo blamed your daughter and her

189

friends for leaving Peter in the woods when he was a boy. But instead of killing them he set this game up to give Peter the opportunity to save them because he wasn't given the chance to save his wife and son. It seems like the whole game was a cathartic exercise to help Peter cope with his grief.'

The Sheriff shook his head.

'So he murders four people, well five if we find that he did kill the person buried in the cabin. And he seriously injures another so she's going to be scarred for life. And he does all of that to try and make himself feel better?'

The doctor didn't know what else he could tell him. He shuffled the paper laid out on the desk into his folder and stood up.

'We won't be able to find out anything else tonight. I suggest we leave him for now and I'll come back in a few hours. I would appreciate it if you or one of your officers could check in on him from time to time. There is the possibility that he could relapse.'

'Yes sure, we'll keep an eye on him.'

They walked out of the room and down the corridor towards the reception area.

'How are you coping with all this?' The doctor enquired.

'I don't know. I don't think it's sunk in yet. I guess I'm just keeping busy and trying to do my job.'

'And how is your daughter doing?'

'I think she's still in shock. I haven't been able to spend much time with her over the last few hours.'

'I understand. You should go and see how she is. It's been a traumatic day for you both. If either of you need to talk to someone about it, I'll gladly help where I can.'

The Sheriff smiled and nodded.

'Thank you. We'll see how it goes.'

He shook the doctor's hand and watched as he left the building. A flurry of camera flashes lit up the entrance to the police station as the journalists gathered outside took photographs of the doctor.

'Fucking vultures.'

He headed down the corridor and went into his office. Michelle was lying asleep on the sofa with her head in Steve's lap as he watched her and stroked her hair.

'How long has she been asleep?' The Sheriff whispered.

'A few hours,' Steve replied.

'Good. And how are you holding up?'

'I can't believe this is happening. That Peter is behind all this. I wish I'd done something.'

'You weren't to know Steven. You did the right thing coming to me and telling me he went into the woods. Otherwise, we might not have found him and who knows what else the bastard could have done.'

'So what's going to happen to him now?'

'I don't know and I don't care. All I care about is making sure Michelle is alright. She's lost her husband and I've lost my son-in-law tonight. But we haven't lost the father of my grandchild.'

Steve looked at The Sheriff in shock. He had no idea that Michelle's father had any knowledge of their affair and he was especially surprised that he had come out with it so bluntly.

'Steven, this is a conversation I was going to have with you anyway. You've been acting like a big kid for most of your life but it's time to grow up now and take responsibility. I need your help to make sure Michelle gets through this. Do you understand?'

'Yes, sir.'

'Good. I have to go and fill out some reports. We'll talk about this more later.'

The Sheriff turned and walked out of the office without waiting for any further response or acknowledgement from Steve.

Peter sat on the bed hugging the quilt tightly and staring blankly at the walls enclosing him. His eyes were bloodshot and exhausted of tears. He thought about all the fences and walls he had climbed over during the course of the day. Those barriers which had been erected to keep the dangerous people out - the monsters like him. All day he had yearned to leave this town and go home but that wasn't going to happen now. He knew where he would be going. An institution which was also likely to have fences but this time they would be designed to keep the monsters in. Maybe that had been Celo's plan after all. There was nothing left outside the gates that he cared about anymore.

Peter felt groggy and the walls surrounding him started to blur. At first he panicked and tried to steady himself, taking deep breaths. Then he wondered if it was Celo. Is this what it felt like when he took control? If so, then why was he fighting it? He wanted the pain and heartache to go away. He surrendered, closed his eyes and drifted off into unconsciousness.

ACKNOWLEDGEMENTS

I would like to thank the following: Craig Alewood, Kate Alewood, Chris Blackwood, Ann Brown (Mi Madre), Kristel Brown, John Dean, Don Elliot (for internally debating whilst dancing on the spot, under a milky dark blue sky), Suzie Evans, Dave Kincla, Jackie Moffat, Kirsty Moffat, Mark Stanton and Sue Vardy.

ABOUT THE AUTHOR

Paul Brown is a Darlington (UK) based author who looks like the monster from the Pickled Onion Monster Munch crisps. I love brown sauce, which means my surname is quite fitting. I have no sense of smell which is also handy because I cover everything I eat with brown sauce.

If you would like to send me any thoughts or comments on the book you can send me a message via Facebook:
http://www.facebook.com/brownybooks

CPSIA information can be obtained
at www.ICGtesting.com
Printed in the USA
FSOW04n2047201217
42658FS